LE FAY

A SOOTHSAYER NOVELLA

ALLISON SIPE

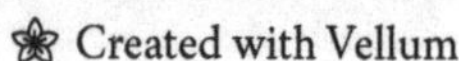 Created with Vellum

ALSO BY THE AUTHOR

SOOTHSAYER SERIES

Soothsayer

Avalon: A Soothsayer Novella

Trivium

Le Fay: A Soothsayer Novella

Elysium

REALMS SAGA

Realm of Flames & Steel

Realm of Stars & Shadows

BOOK PLAYLIST

If you like to listen to music while you read, then you're in luck! We've created a playlist just for Le Fay on Spotify and you can listen here:

To all the Smarter Artists,
Each and every one of you has helped me,
Encouraged me and inspired me to be the writer I am!
You guys are rock stars and
I'm so happy to be a part of the club.

"All the world's a stage,
And all the men and women merely players..."
-William Shakespeare

DAY 1

Whispers filled my ears, calling to me in a primal, visceral way I could feel in my bones. My chest gave a gentle squeeze, and the unmistakable thrum of my heartbeat crashed against my rib cage. It had been eons since I last felt the cadence of the organ in my chest. As the whispers grew louder, almost deafening, blue tendrils of light snaked their way toward me.

"What is this?" I said under my breath.

Blue light wound its way around my wrists and up my arm, burning my skin with agonizing heat. I dared not to scream out in the fear that Vivian might gain pleasure in my pain. This had to be her doing, some fresh, new kind of torture.

Tendrils of light converged on each other until I could see nothing but a bright blue hue swirling around me in a fire that tore at my soul. My heart battered against my chest, leaving me breathless as the light burned my eyes. The gown I'd been wearing for centuries tore off of me, piece by piece, exposing my delicate skin to the heat of the lapping vines of light. The whispers grew louder, and lightning crackled around me and danced across my skin. A crisp, sharp scent filled my nose. A fragrance I hadn't enjoyed for centuries. Fresh air.

My eyes snapped open. Before me, a rippling mirror reflected the world I'd lost when Vivian dragged me beyond The Veil. Orange flames reached for the midnight sky just on the other side. The thick smell of ash mingled with the damp, salty air. I took a hesitant step toward the reflection, unsure if I should trust my eyes. The whispers filled my ears, calling me forward, and the pain subsided with each step I took toward the looking glass. Reaching up, my fingers danced across the surface of the image, creating a ripple effect like a pebble thrown into a pond.

Pulling my fingers back a fraction, I wondered if, like a pebble, I could fall through the surface. As I pressed my palm against the world I was forced to leave behind, a flutter of excitement ran through me. My fingers disappeared into the reflection, and I could feel the wind on my fingertips. Another flash of lightning erupted from the coils surrounding me as I took a step forward.

My foot passed through and landed on something soft and damp. The long-forgotten tingle of my Magic crawled over my skin, forcing me to close my eyes in ecstasy. Drinking in my Magic felt like having a sip of ale after a bout of abstaining, and I needed more. Pushing myself the rest of the way through, my Magic roared to life, and the whispers died as they said my name one last time. All the pain and heat vanished. I was solid, alive and powerful for the first time in many moons.

A man rushed toward me and handed me a cloak to cover my bare body. The cool temperature nipped at my exposed skin and it took a moment for my eyes to adjust after the brilliance of the cobalt luminescence that afforded me passage here. Magic coursed under my skin, eager and hungry for the taste of release after centuries without use. My eyes searched the men and women standing before me when I felt the unmistakable eyes of a traitor. Looking up at the trees in the distance, my eyes blurred as I tried to focus on the two traitors hiding amongst the trees, watching us like rats. Without a word, I raised my arm and pointed a finger in their direction. Everyone's heads followed the point of my index finger and then a man began barking orders.

"After them," he yelled, and several of the figures in the shadows turned and ran toward the two vermin hiding in the bushes. "Ian, find her and bring her to me," the man snapping orders grabbed one of the men, whose face was hidden by the flicker of the flames. He felt familiar as he tore off into the night, but with my Magic newly returned, I couldn't quite work him out in the brief moment I had to focus on him.

Taking a step forward, my legs wobbled, and I fell to my knees. It had been too long since I'd felt the weight of a corporeal form.

"My lady," the one barking orders approached me. "Allow me." He dropped to his knee in front of me and bowed his head.

Nodding my consent, I took his hand and allowed him to pull me to my feet. Leading me slowly away from the platform of my rebirth, he said, "It's a great honor to welcome you back to the land of the living."

"And just who exactly is it that achieved the impossible?" I huffed as another wave of Magic coursed through me.

"Of course, where is my head?" He tapped my hand in an over-friendly way. "My name is Aiden Patridge. Generations of my family have dedicated their lives to returning you to your rightful place."

"And it would appear that you were the one capable of accomplishing such a feat."

He looked up at me from beneath long lashes and smiled. "Nothing's impossible if you believe in what you're fighting for."

"So it would seem." It had been centuries since I interacted with the living, but I was fairly certain his overzealous attitude was meant to impress me.

It didn't.

With each step, my legs grew stronger. But still, I kept my arm safely in the crook of his. Showing any sign of weakness would only serve to undermine me in the long run.

"I've arranged a room for you. I'm sure you'll be wanting some privacy," he said as a structure came into view. The stones of the outer walls look smooth and well finished, and the surrounding landscape was polished.

This will do nicely, I thought, as a smile played on my lips.

"Yes, privacy would be greatly appreciated after tonight's exploit."

His muscles were tense as he guided me into the manor. I could tell he was brimming with centuries worth of anticipation, but he restrained himself, which I respected. A man who didn't know how to temper his emotions, was no man at all. Unfortunately, the same couldn't be said about the men and women, gawking and whispering as we passed.

"Emilia dear, will you show Morgana to her room?" Aiden said when we reached the bottom of the staircase.

"Of course, Sir." Her eyes stay glued to the floor, and she bobbed her head.

Detaching myself from Aiden, I looked between him and the girl. With my Magic becoming stronger with each passing moment, I could distinguish that she was Magical. A ribbon of fear and anger pulsed through her as Aiden stood before her. She disliked him, and it was personal.

Glancing in Aiden's direction, I sensed an air of secrecy around him. He was not the man he pretended to be in this moment. He wanted power, my power, and that just wouldn't suit me.

I gave Aiden a curt smile and nodded for Emilia to lead the way.

Following her up the stairs took more energy than I remembered, but I took pleasure in each breath of air, each extension of muscle. I'd never fully appreciated how luxurious it was to have skin that could feel the grain of the wood and bones that cracked with each step. To take a breath and smell the tangy sweat of men, the sweet aroma of meat cooking in the distance and the fragrance of the floral arrangement placed at the top of the stairs. How truly wonderful and precious it was to be alive again and feel my blood pumping through my body.

Emilia opened a door on my right. "You're shivering. Can I get you something warmer to wear?"

"So I am." I examined the gooseflesh across my arms. "A warm bath will do." I looked around the room for a washing basin but found only a large bed and wardrobe.

"The washroom is just this way." She motioned for me to follow her further into the room. Around the corner of the wardrobe was a small hallway leading to a washing tub and basin. "Would you like some assistance, My lady?"

"You may call me Morgana."

Emilia gave me a small smile, her amber hair falling across her eyes as her cheeks flushed a rosy shade of pink.

"And yes, I would appreciate your assistance. It would seem that the world has evolved without me."

"Allow me to show you." Emilia demonstrated how the water flowed from the outside into the house with just a flick of her wrist. The world had changed while I was away. Life seemed less complicated with basic needs being delivered with a simple twist of a knob. One could hope the Magical world had evolved just the same.

"Tell me, Emilia. Is Magic accepted in this world? Do you not have to hide your true self anymore?"

Emilia's eyes met mine for the briefest of moments. "I'm afraid not much has changed in that regard. We must hide our true selves, our Magical selves from the rest of the world. Most have forgotten that Magic is even real, they believe it's just a folktale." A scowl played across her features, pulling at her brow as she explained. Even without the gift to read one's emotions, it was clear she detested those who forced her to hide who she really was.

She was exactly the type of woman I wanted by my side. She needed to be free of the shackles that bound her and kept her obedient. There was a flame within her belly that I believed I could spark into a full-blown inferno under the right circumstances.

"Shame," I said, keeping my voice light and dropping my robe.

Emilia turned away at my naked skin and said, "I'll just be outside your room if you need anything."

"Thank you, Emilia." I stepped into the steaming water without so much as a glance backward.

There were many trials to come over the next few days, and it was best no one got too comfortable around me in the meantime.

Sliding into the warm water, I shivered as the heat sloshed around me. Submerging myself from the neck down, I lifted my right arm, letting droplets of water crawl down my fingers and drip off the edge of my nails. Testing my Magic, I focused on the next droplet of water, just barely hanging onto the tip of my finger. As it fell, I stopped it mid-air, keeping it suspended.

Closing my eyes, I let the droplet plunge toward my leg, along with my hand. Focusing on every molecule of water that caressed my skin, I released the Magic burning inside me slow and steady. The liquid bubbled around me, growing warmer and warmer as each wave of Magic rolled off of me.

Without much effort, I let my Magic take over and opened my eyes. Streams of water reached for the ceiling and swirled above me as if it was dancing to the cadence of my Magic. As I stood in the now empty basin, I stepped under the droplets, allowing them to fall on me like rain on a spring morning.

Letting my head fall back, I shivered in pleasure as the water dripped into the dark tendrils of my hair and continued down the length of my body.

I was alive.

DAY 2

My Magic had returned while I was asleep and I was feeling much more like myself. I could taste its power once more as I stood on the balcony looking over the foyer, observing the comings and goings of Aiden's soldiers. They listened to his every word, his every command like good little lap dogs. Their minds would be easy to mold, and they'd fit into my plans nicely.

As I scanned the faces below me, my eyes landed on a tall, lean man. His short blonde hair shone like a beacon among the otherwise mundane group of men huddled around Aiden. Dirt blotched his clothes, and he looked as if he hadn't seen his bed last night. As I watched him, he ran a hand through his unkempt hair. The absent movement struck me as familiar and a tingling sensation formed in the back of my mind. I knew him, but how?

The man spoke with Aiden in hushed tones as I descended the staircase one step at a time, training my ears to their words.

With each step, the flutter of familiarity grew in my chest. My eyes traced the length of him, studying his broad shoulders, the curve of his jaw. *It couldn't be, after all this time?*

8

"Don't blame yourself for my daughter's lack of judgment." Aiden reached out and clamped his hand over the blonde man's shoulder. "We'll deal with her when the time comes."

"And the Healer?" He lifted his head, and I caught the sharp edge of his profile. It had been so long since I'd seen a friendly face, it sent a thrill through me to know I wasn't alone in this world.

"I give you my word, Ian, no one but you will strip him of his life."

Ian nodded, and a small smile played on his lips.

"Sir, we have an update for you on the wards when you're ready." A tall, tightly wound woman interrupted any further conversation with the man I sought.

"Ahh, Morgana," Aiden said as he turned to leave. "I was hoping to speak with you this afternoon."

"I'm still adjusting to all of this." I motioned with my hand. "I'd prefer to speak, when I'm feeling more myself." In reality, I didn't want to speak with him at all until I determined his value.

"Of course," he smirked. "Ian, make sure Morgana is well-taken care of in the meantime."

"Without question," he said.

Aiden looked up at me, beaming with delight. I nodded and gave him a tight smile in the hopes he would sense his dismissal.

"Shall we?" Aiden said to the Amazon woman, and they walked out of sight.

"Mordred?" His name rolled off of my tongue and I delighted in the way his shoulders stiffened.

"No one's called me by that name for centuries, my queen." A crooked smile touched his lips as he looked up at me. His name may have changed over the centuries, but the man looking back at me would always be my Mordred.

"After all this time?" I said, studying his features as I came to a stop in front of him. Looking up into his eyes, he was much taller than I remembered. Tentatively, I reached out and touched his face with the tips of my fingers. "You've changed." I gave him a hesitant smile and let my hand fall to his chest over his heart.

"As have you."

Pulling my hand away from him, I folded my arms over my chest. "How've you come to be here?"

His eyebrows shot up as he looked over my features.

"Did you really think I'd ever stop fighting for you?" He asked in a measured and even voice.

My lips threatened to crack a smile as I took in his earnest words. I knew the truth of his heart better than anyone, but I was surprised that he'd speak so candidly about his loyalty while his allegiance seemed to be with Aiden.

"It would appear not, but appearances can be deceiving. The company you keep is provocative, to say the least." I looked in the direction Aiden had gone.

"One must do what is necessary in times of great need." His eyes darted to the huddle of Aiden's followers a few feet away. "I'd like to show you something. If that's all right." He held out his arm for me.

"Of course." I snaked my arm through his. Feeling the warmth of another person intoxicated me after spending so much time alone in the darkness. "And if you don't mind, I'd like to ask you a few questions about your leader," I said under my breath.

"I'd be happy to share my thoughts with you, some place a little more private." His voice was soft, which piqued my interest. "And, you should put this on." He handed me a thin metal bracelet.

"What's this?" I slipped the jewelry onto my wrist.

"It'll keep the Soothsayers blind to your plans."

"If only we'd had this before," I said under my breath.

I could feel the ache in his heart as if it were my own. I may have spent the last few centuries beyond The Veil, but he had been alone with the memory of that fateful day.

"What happened is behind us, we can't allow the pain to rule our present," I mused.

He pulled me closer to his side. "Your Magic has returned to you fully, I see."

"Even if my ability to sense another had been lost, I'd always know what you're feeling. Your face is an open book, my dear Mordred."

"Most would disagree with you." His eyebrows shot up as he glanced at me.

"Then they must not know you well."

A comfortable silence settled over us as he led me through the entry and out onto the pristine lawn.

My eyes darted around the grounds, taking in everything around me. The blue, gray sky, the birds, the sharp green of the trees surrounding us. It was sensory overload, and goosebumps crawled across my skin as a breeze rustled my hair. The centuries I'd spent beyond The Veil had left its mark on me, changed me forever. I wondered if Mordred could see the difference. If he could see the darkness that haunts my soul.

Leading me deeper into the woods, the trees, and the damp smell of dirt and leaves reminded me of home. With each step, I could feel excitement starting to bubble up inside Mordred as we moved further away from prying eyes. The familiar tenor of his emotions was soothing, and a comfort to know some things stayed the same.

"We're almost there." He gave me a small, secretive smile.

Letting go of my arm, Mordred took a few steps into a small empty clearing. He reached into his trousers and pulled out a handful of stones.

"Elemental stones," he said, holding his hand out for me to inspect them.

Plucking a stone from his hand, the smooth worn surface was warm between my fingers. I recognized the symbol engraved on the surface, but I didn't understand what he planned to use it for.

"The fire stone," he said, taking the stone from my hand and placing it at his feet. "Born out of the flames of a battle won."

Moving a few paces away, he placed the next elemental in the damp earth.

"The stone of air, forged by the last breath of a pure soul," he continued.

I watched him move in a careful circular path as he lay the next stone in the dirt.

"The earth stone," he held the element up for me to see. "Created with the soil from a King's grave."

Completing the circle, he placed another stone. "The water stone, forged in the liquid that graced the inside of the Holy Grail."

The four stones pulsed with an iridescent purple and green light as Mordred pulled a final stone from his pocket. In the center of the clearing, he rolled the stone between his fingers. He looked at me, his eyes glassy as his gaze traced my face.

"The Time stone, born from the blood of someone who exists outside the grip of time. Someone like me, like you."

His lips curled up at one corner, and he beckoned me forward.

Moving to his side in the center of the circle, I kept my gaze on the glowing elementals.

When I reached him, he said, *"Cor Revelare."* The Time stone came to life, shining brilliantly along with the other stones.

Four walls shimmered around us as the forest outside disappeared. As I watched in amazement, the interior of a cabin became solid and real.

"Nimue's?" I brushed my fingers over the familiar wood table in the middle of the room.

The pungent aroma of herbs assaulted my senses, along with the smell of earth and freshly cleaned linen. It was exactly as I remembered it. A small bed nestled in the far corner of the room. A large kitchen table taking up the bulk of the space, a cauldron just to my left and spell books, tools, and jars preserving the most delicate ingredients speckled the table. It was as if Nimue just stepped out to gather herbs from her garden, and at any moment she'd come humming through the door.

"It is," Mordred said with a smile in his voice.

I could feel his emotions well up and match my own, a combination of love and loss.

"I thought you might enjoy a little piece of home in such a foreign world."

"But how?"

"The day Nimue died-"

"You mean the day she was murdered," I snapped back.

"Yes," he cleared his throat. "I cast a spell suspending the cabin in time so it could be reconstructed at a time of my choosing."

"And you chose now, for me?" My heart gave a gentle squeeze at the gesture. Even after all this time, he was putting me and my needs first.

"As they say, there's no time like the present."

"Does anyone else know about the stones?"

"Of course not. If Aiden had any idea the elementals existed, he'd abuse their power."

Moving through the cabin, I inspected the books laid open on the table and opened bottles of long-preserved herbs, breathing in their earthly scent, my heart threatening to beat out of my chest with happiness. I hardly dared to dream I'd ever be free from The Veil, let alone have a piece of my home back.

"Speaking of Aiden," I began. "Do you think I should spare him?" My eyes trailed up and down the length of him. A test to root out his true loyalty. Mordred was once my most trusted ally and lover, but time changes everyone.

"No." His voice was cold and hard.

"Would you so easily turn on someone you've been loyal to, *Ian?*" I used his adopted name like a curse, and he flinched at the acid in the moniker.

"I'm not loyal to Aiden." He took a measured step toward me. "I've been loyal to the Patridge family because they were easy to manipulate and mold. Freeing you from the grips of The Veil, restoring your throne, that's where my loyalty lies, always has."

He reached for my hand and I let him take it. His emotions did nothing to betray his words, proving he was still my Mordred.

"Very well then," I said. The tension in his shoulders visibly eased. "It's settled. He'll either take his place at my feet, or he'll be shown the blunt edge of a sword."

Mordred's icy blue eyes met mine, and I felt the thrill of vengeance rise within him.

"If you don't mind me saying so, he shouldn't be given a choice. He isn't loyal to you or your cause. Aiden only cares about collecting power."

"I've gathered that." I pursed my lips and thought of Emilia and the way she recoiled from Aiden. "And what of his followers?"

"Some are fiercely loyal to him, others I believe you can sway in the right direction."

"I trust you can assemble any sympathizers to my cause?"

"Of course," he nodded. "How soon do you want to gather them?"

"As quickly as we can. I need to solidify my position with a show of strength."

"Tomorrow then."

"Time to show them who their real master is." With each

word, I could feel my strength, power, and passion return to me. It had been too long since I'd felt capable.

"I have no doubt all will kneel at your feet in no time." He leaned against the counter and folded his arms over his chest. "But there's something you need to be aware of." His eyes fell to the floor.

"I'm listening." I folded my hands in front of me.

"There's a woman named Violet Evans." The girl's name rolled off the tip of his tongue as if it left a filthy taste in his mouth. "She's destined to wake Vivian and send you back beyond The Veil. Arthur's kin have her under their protection."

I balked at the mention of my brother's name, but quickly composed myself. "Even from the grave, Arthur manages to stand in my way. No matter, I'll take care of the whelp."

"You can't." He forced the words out.

"Excuse me?" I rounded on him. My brow furrowed and my teeth ground together.

"After our last attempt on her life, Alyssa, our researcher, came to me with a script on the Shadowlands. It's possible we can save Nimue, but we need Violet to do it," he blurted.

"Care to explain?" I said through gritted teeth.

"The prophecy explicitly states that Violet is the key to waking The Lady of The Lake," Mordred emphasized the moniker.

"That title was lost when Nimue and Vivian's soul split." Realization settled in my heart.

"I know." The corners of his lips rose.

I paced the kitchen again. "You think she may be able to call on Nimue in the Shadowlands and Vivian beyond The Veil and reunite them," I said, more as a statement than a question.

"I don't know," he shook his head. "All I can say for certain is The Lady of the Lake is both Vivian and Nimue. If there was ever an opportunity, this is it."

"How is she to wake The Lady?"

"Vivian left tokens behind that are linked with her soul. When Violet has all three tokens, she'll be able to call upon Vivian."

"Then we must alter these tokens, so they call upon Nimue instead."

"That's easier said than done." He ran a hand through his golden locks.

"What aren't you telling me?"

"It was Merlin who cast the spell, binding Vivian to each of the tokens."

I sighed. "So we can't break the spell."

Mordred's lips formed a hard line, and he shook his head.

"Then we'll need to dream up a way to alter the intention of the spell."

A dry scoff escaped his throat. "You think I haven't been trying to find something, anything? It's an impossible situation." He rubbed the back of his head.

I stopped in my tracks and turned to face him. "Some said my return was impossible, but here I stand."

"True."

"Then anything is possible, and we will save Nimue."

"I've missed your tenacity." Mordred's eyes caught mine, narrowing at the sides as a devilish smile pulled at his features.

"First, I need to know everything about these Tokens, the spell Merlin cast and how they're linked to Vivian. Once we have a better understanding of how they work, then we can attempt to alter them to our means."

"I can get you anything you need." He pushed off the counter, his shoulders back and his eyes focused.

"And what about this Violet woman, is she capable? Powerful enough to bring them back?" My voice betrayed my curiosity as I leaned across the table.

"Not yet, she only just came into her Magic recently. A novice at best."

"Then she'll need training, won't she?" I smirked. "And I know just how to give it to her."

DAY 3

The afternoon sun cast a golden hue across Nimues's cottage as I woke to the familiar sharp scent of sage and pine. It seemed like it was just yesterday I was learning how to mix potions, identify herbs and control my Magic right in this room. An unfathomable amount of time had passed, and still, everything looked just as it did in my memory.

Mordred left shortly after our conversation yesterday to gather up any support he could muster. He seemed hopeful, but he didn't have the ability to sense the blind loyalty most people here carried for Aiden.

Opening the wooden trunk at the foot of the bed, the metal hinges squealed in protest. Quilts and extra bedding sat inside, and I carefully emptied the contents. As I emptied the chest, my fingers struck the small hand carved box I was looking for. Mordred never knew I'd found his little treasure chest, and it warmed my heart to see it again.

I sat on the edge of the bed and pried the small box open with delicate fingers. There were scrolls of paper, rolled and tied together with string, a small hand-carved bird, and a pendant with the Pendragon seal. I'd once been proud to wear my family's coat of arms, that was of course, until they betrayed me, and exiled me from Camelot. Arthur and his court painted me as a monster, a witch who would stop at nothing to have the throne.

Arthur's story wasn't entirely false. Camelot was meant to be mine as the eldest Pendragon. But when Merlin swept in with Arthur and that damn sword, everything changed. I may not have been able to claim the throne that was rightfully mine then, but nothing would stop me from succeeding this time.

Plucking a piece of twine from the wooden box, I slipped the pendant onto the thread and tied it around my neck, thankful the twine was long enough to allow me to slip the Pendant under my garments and away from questioning eyes. This time, the coat of arms would serve as a reminder not to make the same mistakes twice. This time, I'd lead my people, all Magical born, out of the shadows and bring Magic to the forefront of society where we no longer have to hide our true nature.

A knock on the door startled me.

My Magic searched out the emotions of whoever was on the other side of the door. A pulse of nervous, friendly energy washed over me and I relaxed.

"Come in," I said, setting down the box and righting myself.

"My lady," Emilia bowed her head as she came through the door.

"Emilia, what are you doing out here?" My brow furrowed as I watched her step through the door. I was still wary of everyone and everything. Even Mordred gave me pause, and he's spent his entire life in dedication to freeing me from The Veil.

"Mordred mentioned you might like some company." She used his given name, albeit her tongue fumbled as she spoke his birth name.

"Did he now?" My eyes traced her face.

"I hope I'm not interrupting," she said, noting the open chest.

"Not at all." I beckoned her forward, and she took a seat at the oversized table in the middle of the room.

I took my place across from her but remained standing. For if she were here for nefarious reasons, I'd be prepared.

"Have you spoken to Mordred then, about your place here with Aiden?" I asked.

If he hadn't trusted her to join us, I didn't want to give her any indication of our plans to overthrow her master. She may harbor a hatred for the man, but hate and mutiny were two very different things.

"Oh yes, ma'am." She dipped her head. "Without question I chose you." A shy smile pulled at the corner of her full lips, and her milky white skin flushed a brilliant red. "What I mean is, I will fight under Le Fay for a better world."

"Tell me something," I mused. "How did you come to be here under Aiden's rule?" I cocked my head to the side and studied her. It was clear by her emotions she feared Aiden and detested working for him. So it begged the question, why stay?

"It was Lila who recruited me." Her eyes fell to her hands resting on the table, and she fiddled with her fingers.

"Lila?"

A flurry of emotions fluttered through her, love, hatred, anger, embarrassment. Only someone a woman truly cared for could make her feel so much with just the mention of their name.

"Aiden's daughter." She hesitated and licked her lips. "At first I was only here for Lila. I didn't care about Aiden's mission to bring you back or anything else." Her eyes flicked to mine and guilt ran through her like a hot sword. "I wanted to be where she was, even if she didn't feel the way I did."

"We've all lost our way when it comes to matters of the heart," I said, trying to placate her.

Everyone wants someone to listen to their stories, and the

more people talked, the more they revealed. So I sat patiently and waited for her to continue.

"It wasn't long after I came to Avalon that I realized all of this is bigger than me or Lila. What you tried to accomplish for the Magical world all those years ago, it's worth fighting for."

"And what was it exactly that changed your thinking, your purpose here?"

Pushing her chair back, she stood and said, "It was Le Fay. Ian… I mean Mordred. He spent a lot of time with Lila, talking to her about Le Fay and the supporters who believed in you all over the world. How you would stop, The Waker and free us all from the chains that bind us." Her cheeks flushed again, this time with passion as she spoke. "One day, he was speaking of Arthur and the intensity in his voice caught my attention. Each word felt like they were crafted for me, and me alone.

"What was it he said about my brother that spurred you so?"

"He said, that Arthur was a great King, but he turned his back on the Magical world in favor of his kingdom. Banishing all Magical born to the shadows and exiling you for showing opposition." She looked up at me then, her eyes soft and gentle. "He said the people bound together, forming a group called Le Fay. They all swore an oath to fight for their right to be their true selves. And you, you fought for them until your last breath."

"You speak with a fervor in your heart that can only be born out of persecution," I noted.

Her eyes fell from mine, and she sat down, biting her lip.

"Being different in a world that craves normalcy can leave one feeling marginalized."

Understanding washed over me, and I moved to her side. She was so much like I once was, young, full of anger and passion for justice. She would do well in this fight, and with the right tutelage, she'd make a fine warrior.

"While Aiden and others strive for power and influence, we will seek to make us all equal, to coax us out of the shadows and demand our rightful place in the world." I laid my arm over her shoulders. "No one should ever have to feel as if they're less for being born with a gift others don't understand."

Emilia smiled up at me, and I could feel her emotions solidify into unbreakable loyalty. With the hatred in her heart and the will of a lion, Emilia would be the perfect snake in their garden.

"Despite everything, I thank my lucky stars that Lila brought me here."

I rubbed her shoulder affectionately, the way Nimue used to do to me, and said, "Well then, how about a little help?"

"Anything, My Lady."

"Emilia, please. It's Morgana."

"Right… Morgana."

"I need help sorting through these bottles. It's vital we replenish anything that's no longer useful. I want everything back as it was and in working order."

"Consider it done." She jumped to her feet and moved around the room with practiced hands. Pulling each bottle from the shelves and piling them on the table, she set to work.

While Emilia worked on our supplies and riffled through the bookshelf, I searched for the Grimoire that Nimue and I made together. Emptying the chest of its contents, there were only bits of string and dust under the bed sheets, so I opted for the stack of books sitting on the floor next to Emilia. If Nimue had cloaked the Grimoire for safe keeping, I might be able to sense its Magic. Tossing a book on medicinal herbs aside, I picked up the chronicle closest to me and opened the front cover. At the top of the page in tiny cursive handwriting were the words, *A battle for the soul of Camelot.*

Reaching for the pendant between my breast, I traced the familiar crest with my fingers, gripping the cool metal with all my might. Someone had written it all down, immortalizing my humiliation.

Slamming the book closed, I said, *"Ignis."* And the book burst into flames.

I heard a slight intake of breath from Emilia, but she wisely kept her comments to herself.

A knock at the door caught our attention, and I realized the sun had long since plunged below the horizon. Illuminator orbs danced around the room, bathing us in an artificial summer glow.

Emilia's jumped up and swiftly opened the door without hesitation, sending a dagger of panic through my heart.

Mordred stepped over the threshold with rosy cheeks and bright eyes, and the tension coiled around my abdomen lessened.

"Time to meet your flock," Mordred beamed at me, and I had to fight the playful retort on my lips.

"How many?" I asked, getting to my feet.

"Oh, come now, and ruin the surprise?" Mordred teased as he held out his arm for me to take.

"You know how fond I am of surprises." My voice dripped with acid as I laced my arm through his.

"Yes, well," He cleared his throat, looking rightfully nervous. "We won't let history repeat itself."

"For your sake, I hope not."

He led me outside and turned to the left. Kneeling down, he picked up one of the Elemental stones, whispering a spell against its surface. The cottage disappeared, leaving Emilia standing in the middle of the clearing looking perplexed. The space looked smaller somehow, as if the clearing had shrunk without a dwelling to keep nature at bay.

"We don't want just anyone stumbling into our little haven, now do we?"

Quickly Mordred gathered the rest of the stones, and we made our way toward the beach. The temperature was downright frigid, and the moisture in the air made me shiver as we moved through the trees. Moonlight broke through the canopy above in patches, allowing just enough light to keep us on the path.

The three of us remained quiet, each with our own thoughts about the journey to come. Emilia, I could feel, was nervous. Mordred bordered on excited and cocky. He thought well of himself now and had grown into the man I'd always known he's become. His years had done him well, and it would take some time for me to shed the memory of the wide-eyed, innocent boy he once was.

It didn't take long before the orange glow of fire became visible just beyond the tree line.

As we reached the shore, two or maybe three dozen eyes swiveled around to stare at me. Mordred had fared well, much better than I could've imagined. I gave his arm a gentle squeeze in appreciation as he moved me to the front of the group and then disappeared amongst the crowd.

With wide, doe-like eyes, Emilia sat down on a carefully placed log, her arms stretched toward the fire. She was nervous, that much was plain for all to see. But I was born for this. Born to lead.

Growing up as a Pendragon, I was taught how to command the attention of everyone around me, how to lull people into the sanctuary of my words. I may be out of practice, but some things in life are deeply ingrained in my soul. No matter how long it had been, I would never lose the ability to stand before my people and lead them to victory.

"You're all here because your loyalties are aligned with something bigger than me, bigger than you, and certainly bigger than Aiden." I rested my hand on Emilia's shoulder as my eyes scanned the crowd.

"I've wanted nothing more than freedom for the Magical world," I continued. "A right, it would seem, that has diminished even further in my absence."

The firelight danced across their skin, throwing shadows across their faces, hiding their expressions from me. If not for my ability to feel the nervous, excited energy bubbling through the crowd, I may not be so confident in swaying them in my favor.

"I don't know how much Mordred has told you," My eyes searched out my confidante before I continued. A rush of whispers went through them as they turned to see the man they called Ian was truly Mordred, the knight who slew my naïve brother. "But tonight, I ask you to join me. That you set aside your allegiance to Aiden and join Le Fay in our quest for freedom. In doing so, you will no longer be forced to take orders from a tyrant. You will no longer be made to shy away from your power."

A few of the men in the group shouted their approval, and I waited patiently for my words to sink in. I'd always had a knack for stirring up a crowd.

"I know some of you have concerns," I continued. "I'm told Aiden is a powerful man who is hell-bent on keeping that power. It puts you in a precarious situation, and I understand if you're hesitant." I paced in front of the fire, pressing as much sincerity into each word as I could muster without sounding false. "But fear not. Aiden will be dealt with in a manner befitting his station," I finished and I could feel the unease and doubt begin to abate.

How quickly the winds can change, I thought.

"And how do we know that you'll be any better than Aiden?" One man scoffed under his breath, and every muscle in my body burned to rip his tongue from his mouth. I took a breath before stepping toward the man who spoke out. The time I'd spent beyond The Veil had taught me patience. A trait this man was lucky I'd developed. In my youth, I would've stripped him of his ability to ever utter another word. But if I were to prove that I was a leader worth following, I'd need to win these people over with a silver tongue.

The whispers grew louder, and everyone shuffled away from the man who'd spoken, to distance themselves from the wrath that was undoubtedly about to come down upon him.

"What is your name?" I asked as I stalked toward him. The rest of the group parted, allowing me access to the man who would serve as an example of how merciful I could be.

"David," he said, clearing his throat.

"David, are you not sick of Aiden's tyrannical rule?"

"Of course, but-"

"You can choose to stay in the situation you're in, or fight for a better one." I came to a stop in front of him, holding his eyes. "Based on what I've seen so far, I doubt you'll get the same choice from Aiden."

His eyes fell to his feet, and I could feel the indecision weigh heavy on his heart.

"What is it you're afraid of?" I lifted his chin with my fingers.

His eyes danced wildly to the men and woman standing on either side of us.

"Aiden gave me his word-"

I laughed, cutting him off. "He gave you his word, did he?" I turned to face the others. "How many of you has Aiden made promises to, made bargains with?"

More than half the people standing in the sand raised their hands, flames brightening their eyes.

"You may not trust me yet," I turned back to David as his eyes landed on the dejected faces of the others Aiden had made promises to. "But can you trust Aiden to do right by you?"

David fell to his knees and said, "I don't know."

Kneeling in front of him, I placed my hand on his shoulder. This couldn't be going better if I had planned it myself. "Choose freedom and stop allowing that sad excuse for a King to have control over your life."

The firelight died down as the others crowded around us, and a damp chill settled over David and me.

"But my sister," David whispered as he looked up into my eyes.

"What of her?" My brows furrowed, and I saw an opening that would win me the heart of everyone here.

"She went missing, a few years back. Aiden promised he'd help me find her. He promised."

"Then we'll find her together," I said, rising to my feet and reaching down a hand for him to grab onto. "I give you my word."

Wide brown eyes stared up at me as he reached for my hand and pulled himself up.

An audible sigh ran through the crowd and relieved chatter took hold of the men and women before me.

Turning to face the others who had circled us, I said, "Tomorrow, with your help, we will take Aiden out of the equation with a show of power."

A roar of approval filled my ears.

Meeting each pair of eyes as I moved through the crowd, I continued. "You will have your lives back," I squeezed the shoulder of the woman closest to me. "No longer will you cower in fear of Aiden's wrath; no longer will you fight his battles." I caught Mordred's eyes, and a swell of emotion hit me like electricity as the corner of his lips turned up. "I will not allow others to force us to temper our Magic to appease the unimaginative." I stepped up onto the log nearest the fire. "With Aiden gone, we'll show the world who we are, and what we can do."

Another roar of approval drowned out the waves crashing on the shore. Motioning with my hands to quiet them, I said, "Wait for my call to arms, for it will be swift and with little warning. Should you speak of this night and betray our cause, you will be made an example of. Do I make myself clear?"

One by one they fell to their knees in allegiance.

"You may take your leave," I announced. Swiftly, each soul of my newly minted Trojan army disappeared into the thicket of trees.

Mordred held out his hand for me to take, and I stepped down off the log.

"That was quite a speech," he said.

"I want David's sister found," I said, keeping my voice low.

"You're going to help him?" Mordred's brow furrowed.

I placed a hand on his chest and bit my bottom lip.

"I want her found. David might be swayed to see things our way after all."

"Have I told you how much I've missed you?" His smile reflected in his eyes and I could feel a warmth settle in my chest.

"Once or twice," I said over my shoulder.

DAY 7

Standing on the other side of the prison bars, I stared at a bloody, beaten woman lying on the floor. Knots tangled her long dark hair, and dirt and grime covered her clothes. Mordred's search for David's sister went off with a hitch, further proving that Aiden never intended on finding her.

"Why are you doing this to me?" Her voice was raspy.

"Many things are necessary in war," I replied. "I do apologize that you're caught up in this. I have nothing against you or your brother, but desperate times call for desperate measures."

"You know, David?" She stood and grabbed onto the bars. "Is he okay?"

"Once this is over, he'll be just fine."

Realization flashed across her eyes, and she stepped away from the bars.

"*Silentium.*"

The girl tried to yell, but no sound came from her lips.

"You won't be speaking anymore, I'm afraid."

The familiar tug of Magic poured out of me as I said, "*Egestas a doloribus inferni.*" Ink black smoke crawled across the floor toward David's sister as she tried to scramble away.

When the spell reached her, it crawled up her legs and around her torso like a snake searching for an entrance. As she tried to scream, the spell slithered into her open mouth and began the process of her painful death. She crumpled to the floor, no longer strong enough to keep herself upright, and her mouth fell open in a silent shriek.

The outer door to the prison opened, and two sets of boots descended the stairs.

I left the girl to her pain and met David and Mordred before they reached her cell.

"Milady," he inclined his head. "What's this about?"

"I'm afraid I have news of your sister."

His eyes danced wildly around the faces locked behind bars.

"It appears Aiden's been lying to you."

"Oh God," he whispered.

"She's been here all along," I motioned to the cell behind me.

He ran past me, but I grabbed his arm and said, "You need to prepare yourself. She's not long for this world."

His eyes were glassy as he nodded his head, and I let go of his arm.

My eyes met Mordred's, and a smile pulled at my lips. Oh, how I loved making my puppets dance.

"Evie?" David's voice cracked. "What has happened to you?" He held onto the bars as if they were a lifeline.

I waved my hand over the lock and the bars slid open, allowing him access to his sister who was now curled into the fetus position against the wall.

Brushing the hair from her face, he said, "It's okay, you're going to be okay now."

"Please, can you help her?" David's eyes reached mine.

"I've already called for Alyssa," Mordred said.

"It's okay, Evie. Helps on the way." He pulled her into his lap and rocked her back and forth.

"I'm so sorry, David." I stepped into the cell and knelt next to him.

"You were right, Aiden must be put down like the animal he is," he growled.

"I promise you, Aiden will pay for this."

Evie coughed, and a mouthful of blood splattered David's clothes. The spell was working, and her body was shutting down. Even if Mordred had called for help, it wouldn't arrive in time.

"Oh no, no, just hold on," David's voice shook as he rolled his sister over. "Please just hold on a moment longer."

She coughed again, body going still, and a stream of blood dribbled out of her mouth.

"She's gone, David," I said, keeping my voice as nurturing as possible.

"She can't be. Please." He pulled her limp body to his chest. "Evie, no," he cried.

"I'm so sorry." I placed my hand on his shoulder.

He let out a guttural cry, tears streaming down his face. I motioned for Mordred to help David to his feet.

"I promise we'll take care of her." I wiped the tears from his face.

"I want Aiden's head on a platter," he growled.

I turned to Mordred. "I think it's time for Aiden to meet his fate."

"I'll send out the call to arms."

"And see to it that he's taken care of." I nodded toward David.

"Of course, My Lady." He bobbed his head once, and he and David left the prison.

Only an hour passed and already Mordred had called a strategy meeting with Aiden and alerted my warriors that the time for justice had come. Evie's body still warm in the prison beneath the house and David's anguish still fresh in his heart.

This should be entertaining, I thought, as I walked up the path to the manor.

My high heels echoed on the marble foyer as I made my way to the drawing room. I could feel a tense silence settle over me as everyone waited. My pulse quickened in anticipation and my Magic hummed under the surface of my skin, ready to put on a show and make Aiden's minion mine.

I alone possessed the ability to free the Magical world from the shadows where they've been forced to hide their true nature out of fear of persecution. No longer will we have to bow to the unworthy; instead, I will show them their rightful place at the top of the food chain. And no one, not even a power hungry fool like Aiden, will stand in my way.

Everyone stood as I entered the room, their eyes trained on the table in front of them. Aiden motioned for me to take my place at the head of the table. To everyone else, he was calm and confident as he stood across from me, but his emotions hit me like a sandstorm, coarse and violent. No one could hide from me, no matter how skilled they might be at hiding their true feelings.

He inclined his head out of duty but kept his eyes raised, unwilling to submit completely. As I took my seat, the others followed suit. Glancing around the room, each man and woman shriveled under my glare.

This was going to be too easy, I thought

"Welcome, Morgana," Aiden said once again too over familiar for my taste. "I trust you're being treated well."

"Quite." I folded my hands, finger by finger, on the table and scanned the room. David stood next to Mordred, a scowl on his face strong enough to light the room on fire.

"Wonderful," he said, taking his seat. "Shall we catch you up on the strides we've made in your name thus far?" His lips curved in a tight, unnatural smile. He was pleased with what he'd accomplished, and it annoyed me how blatantly he needed to stroke his own ego.

"While I appreciate your commitment," I purred and picked up the teacup in front of me. "I must ask why you brought me back. It takes someone with more than just commitment to want to pay the price for my soul." I took a sip of the warm liquid. My senses delighting in the perfect balance of robust and light herbs.

"I wanted to help you get back what you've lost." Aiden broke my reverie.

"And what is it you think I lost?" I cocked my head and studied the current of his emotions as I waited for him to answer.

"Your freedom, your throne, the ability to use Magic without persecution," he said with as much authority he could muster into his voice.

"Indeed." I nodded and leaned back in my chair. Clicking my nails on the edge of the chair arm, I let his words hang in the air before asking my next question. "What's in it for you?" I leveled my gaze at him, and a visible shiver ran down his spine.

"I believe in the world you were trying to create before it was taken from you."

"What do you know of the world I fought to protect?" I slammed my hands on the table and rose to my feet.

Aiden stood as well in an attempt to match my strength with his false bravado.

"I know quite a bit, actually," he said and slid a leather-bound tome across the table.

Keeping my eyes on him a moment longer, I looked down at the tightly wrapped Grimoire sitting just an inch from my teacup. Had Nimue not imbued the pages with Magic, surely they would've turned to dust centuries ago.

Gently, I let my fingers trace the smooth, leather symbol on the cover before picking it up and unwinding the strap that contained Nimue's most precious spells and secrets.

"Where did you get this?" I turned the pages delicately. The last time I felt the weight of these pages in my hand, Merlin was hunting me.

"I have a few tricks of my own." His eyebrows shifted on his forehead and confidence rolled off him in thick, hot waves.

"And you read everything, did you?" I fixed my gaze on his stormy blue eyes.

"Yes." A flurry of anxiety whipped through his heart. "It's how I first learned we could rescue you from beyond The Veil."

"Do you take offense to any of the words you've read?" I closed the book and set it back down on the table.

"Of course not, Morgana." His tongue fumbled the four short words.

Picking up the teacup, I returned to my seat, draping myself over the pathetic dining chair and making it my throne.

"And what of your men?" My eyes moved around the room. "Do they take issue with any of my ideals?"

"They are entirely loyal to me. You need not worry about them."

"Ahh, but I do," I leaned forward. "For they need to be loyal, to me."

"I will do anything you ask, and in turn so will they," Aiden said, trying to abate any concern.

"I don't need them to follow your orders; I need them to follow mine." Standing again, I circled the table. I let my hand graze the shoulders of each man and woman I passed, sniffing out my target. I bit my bottom lip as I felt my victim warm under my fingertips.

I placed both of my hands on his shoulders and leaned in. As my cheek brushed his, I whispered, "I want you to kill Aiden. Right here. Right now."

The man's body stiffened under my grasp, and I could feel cold, sharp terror grip his soul.

"You can't be serious?" He stuttered.

"Do it," I snarled. Gripping his shoulders tightly, I forced him to stand up.

"I... I-" one hand still on the table, his eyes shifted from me to Aiden.

"Stop your muttering and do as I ask," I growled. He was a terrified little pup, and I knew he wasn't going to kill Aiden.

His knees shook as his eyes landed on Aiden apologetically.

"Wait a minute," Aiden said, looking between his loyal guard and me. "What did she ask you to do?" Fear bubbled inside of Aiden as realization set in.

"Strike now or seal your own fate." My voice was laced with venom.

The guard hesitated, and it was time to show them who they were dealing with. Turning away from the traitor, I felt a sense of relief wash over him as I made my way back to my end of the table. I let him relish in his freedom for just a second longer, then raised my hand in the air and closed my fingers into a tight and unrelenting fist. The guard who failed to follow my orders gasped for air, clawing at his neck as an invisible force crushed his airway.

As I took my seat, I looked directly at Aiden and smiled. Twisting my closed fist, the guard's body slammed onto the table, rattling the china as the life drained from his eyes.

"So you see, your men are not loyal to me." I picked up my teacup and sipped gently. "And that just won't do."

Aiden stood, cleared his throat and asked, "How do you suggest we remedy the situation?"

"I need to form my army, choose my allies. You have done me a great service, but I fear your usefulness has come to an end." Leaning back, I could feel the waves of anxiety rolling off him as I nodded my head once.

Mordred put his hand on Aiden's shoulder and forced him to his knees.

"Ian?" Aiden Whimpered.

"The name's Mordred."

Realization flashed across Aiden's face, and his eyes darted to me as Mordred withdrew a dagger.

"You think I'm just going to let you kill me, in my house?" Aiden spat at Mordred and struggled to his feet.

"Now's your chance," I said, addressing the others in the room. "To prove where your loyalties lie."

Without hesitation, a young, lanky fellow in the corner stepped up. With a Binding spell he forced Aiden to his knees in one swift motion. Now that it was clear the tables had turned, another cast a Silencing spell, keeping Aiden's cries from reaching our ears.

"Do it," I egged them on.

Mordred pushed Aiden's head back with one hand and carved my symbol into his forehead. Blood dripped down Aiden's cheeks, and while the room was silent, a torrent of emotions bounced off the walls. Fear, excitement, dread, and eagerness swirled around me. I felt an unabashed thrill run through me and realized it was coming from the archway to my right. Glancing in that direction, I noticed Emilia's face huddled behind a man twice her size. Her eyes beamed bright with excitement, and her heart pounded in a frenzy as she watched.

Mordred pulled Aiden's head back, exposing his bare neck. Flipping the knife with skilled hands, he held the hilt out to David.

Stepping forward, he grabbed the knife and stared down into Aiden's eyes.

"This is for Evie," David growled and slit Aiden's throat from ear to ear.

I watched my predecessor's body slump to the floor, blood pouring from the wound on his neck.

"Thank you, David." I nodded in approval. "Now for those of you who haven't already pledged your allegiance to me," I paused, waiting for everyone's attention. "Now is your opportunity to choose which side of history you'll be on."

Mordred moved to stand behind me, clearly showing his support. Quickly the support of Emilia and the others who met me on the beach followed suit. With the line in the sand drawn, a tense silence settled over the room like a thick fog. Half a dozen people stayed huddled next to Aiden's body, a choice they would soon regret.

"Very well then, the rest of you-"

"I warned him that you would be a curse on us all." A woman kneeling next to Aiden screamed. His blood dripped from her fingertips as her own flushed her cheeks.

"I'd bite my tongue if I were you," Mordred warned.

Spitting in Mordred's direction, she said, "I'd rather die than bow to a false Queen."

My fingers itched with the urge to let my Magic grant her wish. Taking a deep breath, I forced myself to swallow my anger, when violent green sparks shot across the room and hit the woman. Looking over my shoulder, I saw that the Galvin spell had come from Emilia.

"After everything Aiden did, you would still choose him over Morgana?" Emilia said through gritted teeth.

The woman's rebuttal was lost in a moan of agony as the spell worked its way into her nervous system and attacked her body from the inside out.

Mordred stepped forward to corral Emilia, but I put my hand out to stop him. The visceral hatred spewing from Emilia toward this woman was personal, and it wasn't for us to meddle in.

"She has a score to settle. Let her," I addressed Mordred, and he stepped back.

"You're just as corrupt as Aiden," Emilia seethed at the woman still holding Aiden's limp body. A cinder orb whirled into existence, and Emilia threw it at the woman, her writhing figure turning to dust before our eyes.

"As I was saying," I said, once again drawing everyone's

attention. "The rest of you have a choice to make. Join me or get out of my way."

The remaining doubters hurried across the room, leaving Aiden's body and the pile of ash lying on the floor alone.

"There are a few matters I must address up front." I turned to face my supporters. "Unlike Aiden, I do not want The Waker killed. Is that clear?" I barked like a general before battle. After all, the soul of the Magical world was a war I intended to win.

A low mumbling of consent rolled through the crowd.

"Our priority is finding The Pieces of Three before Violet and her merry band can get their hands on them. Mordred will lead the charge on their whereabouts. Should you come into the possession of any knowledge regarding the Tokens, it is imperative you let Mordred know at once.

"Now, I'm told that Aiden kept order with some sort of hierarchy. I would like to meet with the top tier directly after this gathering."

I stepped up onto my chair so all could see me speak my next words. "For some of you, the oath you made to me was an easy choice. Others will struggle with their allegiance. Regardless, I make this oath to all of you. Unlike Aiden, I will fight alongside you as long as I have breath in my lungs and blood in my veins." Their eyes watched me as I drove my message home. "This world is ours. No longer will you be relegated to the outskirts of society. Now is the time for justice, to stand up for Magic and show everyone how resilient we are."

Electricity crackled across my fingers, begging to be released. The room swirled with everyone's emotions; elation, fear, excitement, and passion.

"For Le Fay," Emilia yelled.

"For Le Fay." A nameless face called out.

Without any more encouragement, cheers, whistles and the ever-present chant, *For Le Fay!* roared through the room.

They were mine

DAY 8

Climbing out of bed, I raised my arms above my head and my spine cracked and relaxed. It had been over a week since my re-birth, and while my Magic was in full working order, my body and soul were still adapting to the weight of the world.

After yesterday's excitement, I decided to stay in the cabin full-time and use the Manor for official matters. The prospect of staying some place so unfamiliar and cold when we had access to Nimue's cabin was absurd. As I sifted through the clothes Emilia had gathered for me, I opted for one of the familiar dresses. Slipping into the emerald green and gold garment with ease, I slid the Pendragon pendant around my neck and beneath the hem of my bust. I took a seat at the table and flipped open the Grimoire Aiden had so arrogantly shoved in my face. Had I not already marked him for death, I would've killed him for daring to lay a finger on Nimue's Grimoire.

Knuckles rasped against the door, making my heart skip a beat as I read over Nimue's words.

"Come in." Mordred stepped into the cabin, and a wave of nostalgia washed over me. If I closed my eyes, I could pretend we were in another life, and Mordred was coming home while his mother and I worked. My heart warmed at the sight of him, and I couldn't help but beam at the memory of the boy I once knew so well.

"Someone's in a good mood this morning," he noted.

"It feels like home." I leaned my head back and closed my eyes.

"That was the idea," he said placing a plate of assorted fruits, bread and what smelled like a smoky, perfectly crisp piece of pig. "Thank you," I said, reaching for a toasted roll.

He pulled out a chair, spinning it on one leg, and sat facing me with his arms draped over the back of the chair. "After reviewing the lack of information we have on Violet and the Maxwell's, I believe I've come up with a plan." I cut the roll in half.

"And what might that be?"

"You said there were two women in the Maxwell family?" I looked to him for confirmation. "I want you to bring one of them here."

Mordred's eyes narrowed, his head falling to one side as he said, "They're not likely to talk if that's what you're after."

"Oh, how narrow-minded you can be." My lips curled into a smile. "With one of them here, we can send Emilia back in their place, disguised as one of their own." Cutting off a piece of the pork and placing it on the roll, I took a bite and closed my eyes in delight. "Bacon," Mordred said. "One of the many improvements in breakfast fare."

"Dare I say, it's even better than the concept of indoor water," I smiled.

"You were saying, a Trojan horse," Mordred popped another grape into his mouth. "How do you intend to cloak Emilia? They'll notice if she puts one toe out of place."

"There was mention of a woman, Alyssa, during the briefing

yesterday. She likes to experiment with Magical abilities, spells and the like."

"She does. Although I've never been privy to her work, I know she's talented."

"I'd like to meet her, see what she can handle."

Mordred pulled a small box from his pocket, and his fingers flew over the brightly lit glass.

"Consider it done," he said, looking up at me and catching my gaze on the box.

"It's a mobile phone, a tool for communication." He placed the contraption on the table.

"I see." I took another bite of the fluffy biscuit and salty bacon. "Speak with Emilia and see if she is amiable to the idea. I believe your influence over the girl with lead her in the right direction."

"Are you sure you want Emilia handling this task?"

"Speak your mind," I said.

"I wonder if her will is strong enough."

"From what I've seen, she's perfect for this. Angry with an axe to grind. Righteous without provocation."

"She's a loose cannon. Emotional."

"Since when is that a bad thing?" I eyed him.

He chuckled and said, "You've clearly already made up your mind, so I'll see to it she agrees to the task."

"Thank you."

The mobile phone buzzed across the wood surface, startling me.

"Alyssa's in her workshop, I can have her meet us-"

"No, I prefer to drop in on her, see what she's tinkering with," I said getting to my feet.

"I'll lead the way."

Each day I left Nimue's cabin, I felt like I was shedding my skin. It was uncomfortable, even grating, but it was necessary. As we rounded the main house, several smaller dwellings came into view on the other side of a large pond. The lack of stone on the exterior made them look naked and unfinished compared to the manor. The bright white facade and dark roofs were in stark contrast to the earth tones of the rest of the keep.

"There's something you should know about Alyssa before you meet her," Mordred called over his shoulder.

"Oh?" My ears piqued at this.

"She doesn't have Magic, per se." He stopped on the path and turned to face me. "But she does have the ability to manipulate it," he said.

"Interesting. And is this a common occurrence in Magical born now?"

"Not exactly. As you know, Promised Ones have the ability to sense and understand Magic, but Alyssa's utterly different. She doesn't have her own Magic, but she can wield it if she takes it from another."

"I shall keep my guard up then."

"She isn't thoughtless enough to pull on your Magic. I just wanted you to be aware," he trailed off and his eyes glazed over. "In case you felt anything off or different," he shrugged.

"I see," I said as he continued up the path. There were two wooden doors spaced evenly apart from each other. Mordred stepped up to the one on the right and lifted his hand to knock.

"You forget the company you keep," I caught his wrist before his knuckles could graze the smooth oak surface. "This is my domain now, and I will not announce myself to anyone." I released his arm, and it fell to his side.

"Of course." He reached for the handle and pushed the door inward. Motioning for me to take the lead, I stepped over the threshold and froze.

Mobile phones triple the size of the one Mordred carried in his pocket lined the wall in front of me. Lights flickered of their own accord, blinking across each of their surfaces. I'd never seen or even dreamed anything like it.

Scanning the rest of the room, three long tables with instruments stood before me. Against the wall to my left, glass jars with herbs and ingredients lined the shelves from floor to ceiling. The long open layout reminded me of Nimue's cottage, but this was far more chaotic and busy. There was no room to breathe and feel the surrounding energy with all the modern equipment covering every surface.

"Hello, Milady." A young, beautiful woman with red frizzy hair and caramel skin moved around the largest table and came forward.

"Alyssa," I replied coolly.

"What is it I can do for you?"

"I've been told you're very gifted with experiments. I'd like to know more about what you do with…" I motioned toward a few of the devices with flashing lights and said, "All of this."

"It would be my pleasure," she smiled. "My main purpose here is to collect Magical gifts and learn how to emulate them." She rounded the longest table and picked up a bottle that shimmered blue and gold. Pulling the top open, a trail of blue smoke wafted out of the bottle, uncoiling like a snake. "I call it Echo. It gives one the ability to mimic another's voice." Alyssa beamed. "Ia- Mordred, will you allow me to demonstrate?" Her eyebrows raised on her flawless skin as she reached toward him.

He nodded his head in consent, and I could feel the energy shift in the room as she pulled on Mordred's Magic.

"*Acidis imitantur vitea*," Alyssa said the incantation.

"Fascinating." I watched Alyssa inhale the blue and gold smoke up her nostrils as I felt Mordred's Magic settle under her control.

"It's a wonderful party trick," Alyssa said with Mordred's voice.

"It's enough to give a man nightmares," Mordred laughed, and Alyssa rolled her eyes playfully.

I felt the bond of friendship pass between them, and I was

glad to know Mordred hadn't spent the last few centuries entirely alone in his quest to save me.

"A trick worthy of a court jester, indeed," I mused. "How long does it last?"

"At the moment," the deep tambour of Mordred's voice altered on Alyssa's lips. The energy in the room shifted once more, and the Magic Alyssa had borrowed from Mordred returned to him.

"An hour, two at most," she finished with her own lyrical voice.

"I'd be interested to see if you could elongate the effects," I said, eyeing the bottle.

Alyssa's little trick would be the first step in replicating one of the Maxwell women.

"It would be my pleasure. I'll work on it and report back my findings at the next council meeting."

"Shall we continue the tour?" Mordred asked.

"There's a matter I wish to share with you first." Alyssa moved toward one of the flashing boxes and her fingers danced over a set of letters.

A picture of a handsome, dark-haired man popped up on the screen along with a series of numbers and words.

"The healer?" Mordred sneered, and I felt a wave of hostility roll off of him. "Did you find something, then?"

"So this is Robert Maxwell," I said softly as I looked at the image on the screen.

"Yes. While Aiden was holding Robert here on Avalon, he allowed me to run a few experiments," Alyssa replied.

"And?" Mordred's voice was gruff and demanding. I hadn't seen this side of him before, and it sent a thrill through me.

"And," Alyssa sneered. "I think I may have reversed engineered his ability."

"Alyssa, you're a genius." Mordred clamped her on the shoulder.

"Don't get too excited. It's just a theory so far. I'll need to test it first."

"Then test it. Handicapping their healer would be a devastating blow to their morale," Mordred smiled.

"Agreed. We need to take them off guard and hit them where it'll hurt the most," I said.

"I'll start today." Alyssa smile didn't reach her eyes. She was sharp, smart, and carried herself well, but there was a defiance in her that made me feel uneasy.

"Anyone still loyal to Aiden is fair game," Mordred said.

"Understood. Is there anything else I can show you?" She asked.

"Your stores," I nodded toward the herbs and ingredients. "Are they well kept?" I asked.

"Of course. A researcher is only as good as her supply." She made her way toward the wall, rolling the front facade aside to reveal a large room filled to the brim with apothecary jars. Willow leaves and lavender hung from the ceiling, allowing them to dry properly. It was the most beautiful thing I'd ever seen.

I stepped into the room, letting my hand graze the labels on the delicate glass jars. There was Honeysuckle, Aloe, Carbo Vegetabilis, Juniper, and dried crickets, to name a few. My heart gave a gentle squeeze, I worried it might be difficult to recreate a number of potions, but with Alyssa's inventory, I'd have no trouble at all.

"How many have access to these stores?" I turned to face Alyssa.

"Just me." She rolled forward on the balls of her feet. "And you. Of course, My Lady."

"Wonderful, I'll send Emilia with a list. If you wouldn't mind helping her."

"Not at all." She inclined her head, and again I felt a defiant streak in her. She didn't like taking orders. Which made me wonder what her relationship with Aiden was like, given he seemed to love giving orders.

"I'd also like you to come up with a Cloaking spell. We'll be needing to sneak into the enemy camp soon, and it would serve us well to hide in plain sight."

Her mouth fell open as if she was about to object, but she thought better of it.

"I'll see what I can dig up. But I'll need more details if I'm going to create the kind of spell you're looking for."

"You have enough to get you started. Impress me." I held her eyes and let the corner of my lips turn into a sly smile.

"If anyone is capable, it's Alyssa," Mordred said, trying to break the tension.

"Your confidence humbles me, Mordred." His name dripped off her tongue like a curse, and I could feel her frustration bubbling just under the surface.

Moving toward the door, Mordred trailing behind me, I said, "I'll be calling on you shortly, I do hope you'll have made some progress." I kept my voice light, but the threat was evident. She may be friendly with Mordred, but she had yet to earn my trust. If she failed to prove herself, then she'd meet the same fate as my predecessor.

DAY 11

A loud bang somewhere within the manor and the distinct sounds of a struggle piqued my interest. I wasn't expecting Mordred back so quickly, and a nervous flutter settled in my stomach at the thought of something going wrong. I pushed through the double doors and made my way to the landing, calm and collected.

"Let go of me." A blond woman growled as she tried to break free from Mordred's grasp on her. I let out the breath I hadn't realized I'd been holding at the sight of him and took in the rest of the scene.

We'd sent a dozen soldiers to collect one of the Maxwells, but there were only three men besides Mordred in the foyer below. All of them looked as if they'd seen better days. Scorched flesh covered the right side of one of the men, and blood dripped down the forehead of another. How powerful were these Maxwells if they could dispatch our troops so easily?

"Struggle all you like, your knack for disappearing is nothing but a memory now," Mordred sneered as the woman's image flashed in and out like a ghost. Studying her, I wondered what gift she possessed. I'd never seen someone's image flicker, as if the binds of this world couldn't hold them.

As she shimmered again, her face distorted into a pained expression as the chains around her wrists flashed a brilliant green, and she collapsed to her knees in solid form.

I descended the stairs, cocking my head to the side as I watched the woman twitching under the control of her chains.

"It worked then?" I admired the view as I made my way down the stairs.

Mordred looked up, smiling from ear to ear. "Worked just like Alyssa said it would. Tapping into her ability wasn't easy, but with the right force, we managed."

Kneeling down, I reached out a finger and tipped her chin upward, forcing her to look at me.

"Annabel Maxwell, as requested," Mordred reported. Gritting her teeth, she ripped her face away from my touch.

I studied her features as she kept her gaze as far away from me as she could. "You are not the kin of my step-brother," I mused. "You've taken on the name of Maxwell, but you belong to another house."

"Why," Annabel breathed. "Did you request me?" She exhaled each word and her body slumped in pain.

Getting to my feet, I said, "I have plans for you, my dear."

I could feel her anger and disgust boil beneath the surface. She called on her Magic again, her energy wavered as she fluttered in and out of focus in agony. I had to give her credit, she knew escape was futile. Yet still, she tried, causing herself an immense amount of pain.

"You're seriously deranged if you think I'd ever help you," Annabel seethed.

"Do you believe you have a choice in the matter?" I cocked my head to the side, amused.

Her eyes fell to the chains wrapped around her wrists, and her hardened exterior wavered ever so slightly.

"I may be your prisoner, but Jake will come after me and when he does-"

"I hope they all come after you." I leaned over so that my face was inches from hers.

Her eyes widened, and a pang of fear ran through her. But she quickly composed herself and lunged toward me.

Before she could reach me, Mordred yanked on her chains and forced her body to the floor with impeccable speed. Stepping on her bound wrists, he pressed down and said, "Try that again, and I'll kill you myself."

Her jaw flexed as she tried to hide the pain Mordred inflicted upon her.

"Maybe she needs some alone time. Lock her up, and I'll speak more with her shortly." I waved my hand, dismissing Annabel and the guards who helped secure her.

"Come with me, Mordred. I'd like a full report of your little adventure." I beckoned for him to follow me outside.

In my short time here, I'd grown fond of walking the grounds at every opportunity. After spending an eternity shrouded in darkness, I relished the ability to feel the salty air caress my skin, to inhale the crisp scent of fresh cut grass and feel my heart pump with excursion.

"I noticed you returned with fewer than you left with," I noted as I made my way in the general direction of Alyssa's workshop.

"We caught them off guard, but they recovered quickly." He shook his head. "They're strong and growing in numbers. There were two more faces I hadn't seen before."

"Not to worry, our numbers will strengthen."

"It's a shame losing good men."

"Mordred, it would seem that time has made you sentimental." I kept my voice light and playful.

"I don't like my time and effort wasted, and every time they kill one of our own, that's years of coaxing and training down the drain."

"That was before. Now that I've returned, we'll replace every man and woman you've lost tenfold."

His lips twitched into a half smile. "Your confidence is unwavering."

"Tell me, how did Violet fare?" I asked, lacing my arm through his.

"We left her unharmed and far better off in her Magic than the last time I saw her." He ran a hand through his hair, and I noticed that he was bleeding at the temple. "If she keeps up at this pace, she'll be ready to wake The Lady when the time comes."

"Then we'll make sure her training continues to be rigorous, won't we?" I stopped on the path and Mordred turned to face me. A wave of his emotions hit me like a sucker punch as his guard fell.

"Something's bothering you, you're uneasy." I searched his eyes.

"Lila, Aiden's daughter-"

"I know who the girl is. What of her?"

"She was my protégé, and we were close in the last couple years." His eyes fell from mine and shame filled his heart. "She was there, fighting alongside them as if…" he trailed off as the cold stab of betrayal bloomed in his chest.

"We can only lead a horse to water, we cannot make it drink." I placed my hand on his shoulder and moved close to him. With the heat of our bodies only inches apart, I could smell the sweat and blood on his skin. A primal hunger stirred within me, and my heart raced as his eyes met mine.

"Of course you're right, it's just a hard pill to swallow," he scoffed.

"Don't let her presence put a damper on an otherwise joyous day." My lips parted as I looked up at him, and the urge to sink my teeth into him nearly took over.

It had been a long time beyond The Veil, I thought.

Gathering my wits, I widened the gap between us and continued along the path that led to Alyssa's open door. Mordred followed behind me, and I could feel him brooding, vengeance pulsing off of him, making my heart race to the cadence of his anguish.

"Wait here," I said to Mordred as we reached the entrance. He leaned against the exterior just to the left of the open door and crossed his arms without saying a word. He was too much of a distraction with the torrent of emotions running through him, and I needed my head clear and concise.

Alyssa rushed to greet me the moment I crossed over the threshold.

"My lady." She nodded her head once. "What can I do for you?"

"How far have you come in creating a Cloaking spell?" I asked, skipping formalities.

Her eyes shifted from side to side, and she said, "To be honest, it's been a struggle without knowing the end game." The defiant streak in her flared as she spoke. "But I was able to manipulate a Mirroring spell that will allow an individual to take on the image of another and-"

"Have you tested it yet?" I interrupted.

She shook her head and said, "I haven't had the opportunity."

"Well, now's the time. Mordred was kind enough to bring us a prisoner we can use to test your experiment." I still didn't want her to know I intend for Emilia to take Annabel's place in the Maxwell family. Alyssa was a wild card. While she had done everything I'd asked her to do, she'd done so with a chip on her shoulder.

Her eyes widened, and I could feel the anticipation rise within her. This was what she lived for, testing her experiments.

"I would also like you to bring the voice mimicking potion with you. Have you had a chance to elongate the effects?"

"Yes, actually," Her eyes brightened as she retrieved the bottle. "I realized that the potion didn't need altering at all," she smiled and shook the contents of the bottle. "We just needed to marry the potion with a spell that would allow the recipient to mimic an individual's voice as long as they remain linked to one another." Her voice was almost lyrical as she spoke. She truly had a unique enthusiasm for her work.

"A binding spell? And it works?" I asked, impressed.

"Of course," she beamed with confidence. "I tested it just yesterday, and the effects didn't fade until we were unbound."

"I'd like to see everything you've accomplished in action. Emilia and our new prisoner will serve as our test subjects."

"Emilia?" Alyssa's brow furrowed.

"She's a willing participant, a trait that seems to be lacking in others." I stared down at her, holding her eyes until she looked away.

"When would you like to begin?" she asked.

"Immediately. Fetch Emilia and meet us in the main prison, I have a message I need to send."

Turning on my heel, I left Alyssa to her work and returned to Mordred.

"Where to?" His eyes glanced at me. The few moments he'd spent alone did wonders for his mood.

"To the prisoner. I think it best we keep Violet and her allies motivated, don't you?" A smile pulled at the corner of my lips.

Mordred returned my smirk as he pushed off the wall. "Hit 'em while they're down." His eyebrows shifted on his forehead as his hand trailed down my spine and settled on my lower back. The first few days after my return, he'd been careful to keep a respectful distance, but not even centuries apart could keep us from falling into old habits.

"Precisely," I said as he led me away from Alyssa's cabin.

Moonlight spilled onto the path in front of us, shading his face from me. Though his mood seemed to have improved, I could still feel his seething anger just beneath the surface as he traced his fingers along my spine.

Neither of us spoke as he guided me across the estate, but a charge began to build between us. I was keenly aware of his movement, the gentle pressure on my spine as he turned me toward the prison, the catch in his breath as his hand moved to my hip, the distinct flair of desire was building in both of us.

Reaching down, Mordred pulled open the prison door and motioned me forward.

The stairs before me were dark, illuminated only by the moonlight. The damp smell of stone and salt wafted in the air as I made my way deeper into the underground prison.

As I passed each cell, the occupants did their best to shrink into the shadows. Annabel, on the other hand, railed against her prison bars as we approached.

"What do you want with me?" Annabel snarled. Her short blond hair matted with blood and sweat, making her look more like a wild animal than a person.

"All in due time." I looked her over, comparing the vitriol hatred inside her with her beauty. Had I not the gift to feel her emotions, I may not see her for what she really is: venomous.

"Yeah, that's what I'm worried about." She rolled her eyes and slumped against the wall furthest from me. "The only reason to keep me around is that you think I'm more use to you alive and I want to know why."

"You're right; I want you alive for now. But tomorrow, next week? Time will tell," I smirked.

The outer door to the prison slammed shut, and a pair of high heels clicked against the concrete.

"Good, we can begin," I said as Alyssa sidled up to Mordred with Emilia behind her.

"Begin what?" I could feel the subtle change in Annabel's emotions from indignation to anxiety. She may give off an air of confidence and strength, but she couldn't fool me.

"I want to send a message. One Violet won't be able to ignore." I leveled my eyes at her.

"Don't you think kidnapping me is enough of a message?"

"Of course not. They must be made to see who they're dealing with."

"Whatever it is you're trying to accomplish, you won't get away with it. Violet will see right through your tricks."

A low chuckle rumbled in my chest, and I said, "Violet will see what I want her to see. Chain her up," I ordered.

Mordred stepped forward, reaching for the Galvin chains to keep Annabel from using her ability. But she was quick. In one swift motion, she spun around Mordred and pulled the chain around his jugular.

Mordred lifted one hand, flicking his wrist and mumbling through a ragged breath as Annabel's body hit the wall with an audible thump. Her head bounced off the stone, and a trickle of blood dripped down the side of her neck.

Good, I thought. The more roughed up she looked, the better my message would be received.

"Really, Annabel, haven't we been through this?" Mordred taunted as he clipped her chains around her wrists.

"Screw you," she screamed as she pushed off the wall and swung her right arm toward Mordred. He caught her fist in his hand and bent her arm backward, forcing her to her knees. Pulling her by her manacles, he dragged her across the dusty floor and looped the chains around a fitting in the stone wall.

"You're just a stubborn as that filthy Healer," Mordred growled.

She thrashed and kicked, trying to break free from his grasp. Little did she know she was playing right into my hands. I wanted Violet to see her pain; I wanted Violet to see Annabel, desperate to escape and unable to.

Mordred waved his hand over the bars, and the barrier fell away. Annabel's chest rose the moment her Magic returned to her, and her image flickered as she tried to escape. Again, the Galvin spell bound to the chains flared to life, and she screamed in agony.

"I didn't realize you enjoyed pain so much," Mordred chuckled.

"If you think I'll ever stop trying to escape, you're sorely mistaken. All it takes is one slip up, and I'm out of here," she bit back.

"I wouldn't count on that," I stepped forward.

Annabel's eyes shifted to me as she pressed herself against the stone wall. She may not have a problem shooting her mouth off to Mordred, but she had the good sense to be afraid of me.

"Shall we begin?" Green sparks formed on my fingertips as I tapped into my Magic.

"Do your worst," she said through gritted teeth.

Extending my fingers, I let my Magic fly from my hand, sharp and feral. The power of the spell hit her square in the chest. Annabel convulsed without making a sound, and her eyes closed tightly as she tried to keep herself upright.

The Magic coursing within me was intoxicating as I stepped out of the shadows. Pushing more power into the spell, I could feel her strength waver, and I delighted in knowing she was moments from breaking. A deep chuckle escaped my throat as her body gave out and she screamed out in agony.

"Had enough?" I smiled down at her limp body.

I nodded in Mordred's direction, and he waved Alyssa and Emilia into the cell.

Breathless, Annabel lifted herself, pushing her shoulder against the wall and raising her chin to look at me. "Violet won't fall for this, she'll know it's a trap."

Reaching out, I pinched her chin between my thumb and forefinger. "It's human nature to want to help someone you care for, even if you know it's a trap." I pressed myself closer and whispered, "The more we torture you, the more she won't be able to ignore your screams."

Utter despair filled her heart as she tore her face from my grasp.

"Alyssa, it's your time to shine," I said, stepping back to allow Alyssa access to her experiment.

"Emilia. If you will," she motioned her forward.

"What is this, more torture?" Annabel's eyes shifted between everyone in the cell as blood continued to drip down the side of her face and onto her clothing.

"First, you'll need to perform a Connection spell to allow her emotions to flow through you," Alyssa placed her hand on Emilia's back and guided her forward.

"Like hell she does." Annabel's fire returned to her as she tried to pull her chains free from the wall.

"You should be thankful we're not here to hurt you." The cadence of Alyssa's voice was one a medicine woman would use with a grieving patient.

"Hurt me all you want, you can even kill me, but I won't let-"

"You don't have a choice in the matter," Emilia silenced her by placing her hand on Annabel's shoulder and forcing her back against the wall.

"*Tiegan mín sáwol eac hie sáwol*," she chanted. Tendrils of light crawled over her skin like ivy and made their way up her arms, extending to Annabel. "*Alǽtan mec áfindan eall breóstwylm fléding geond hie*," she finished reciting the spell. A soft silvery light wrapped around both of them, coils dancing up their arms, forming intricate patterns until they coalesced over Annabel's heart, then quickly receded and disappeared into Emilia.

"Now drink this and say the spell," Alyssa handed Emilia the Echo potion and a piece of paper.

"*Acidis imitantur vitea*," Emilia said.

Emilia's eyes widened as the spell took hold and Annabel's emotions became her own.

"Go ahead, say something," Alyssa encouraged.

"What should I say?" Emilia's voice was no longer her own.

"What in Merlin's name have you done?" Annabel said through gritted teeth.

"It really won't wear off?" I asked, still unsure of Alyssa's capability.

"As long as the Connection spell holds, Emilia will speak with Annabel's voice."

"Jake will never fall for your parlor trick," Annabel spat.

"Jake will never fall for your parlor trick," Emilia mimicked perfectly.

Mordred's chest rose as he chuckled. "I don't think your mother could tell the difference, let alone that husband of yours."

"The likeness is uncanny," I said.

"Don't you worry." Emilia leaned in close to Annabel. "I'll take good care of your Jake," she whispered in Annabel's lyrical voice.

"So that's your end game," Alyssa turned toward me, a sly smile pulling at her full lips. "Turn Emilia into Annabel and send her into the lion's den?" Her eyebrows rose on her forehead and I could feel her interest in the project pique.

"Yes," I conceded. "I'll need you to find a way to complete the transformation physically."

"I know the perfect spell." She turned to face Annabel.

"I won't be a part of your games." Annabel thrashed against her chains trying to rip herself free. "You can't do this," she yelled and kicked toward Emilia and Alyssa.

Summoning a stunning orb, I lobbed it at Annabel, and her body went limp, silencing her protests. "That's just about all the whining I can handle for one day."

"I'll need to collect some samples from the prisoner before I can start working on the spell to cloak Emilia."

I waved my consent and said, "Do what you must, I want Emilia ready as soon as possible."

"It should only take me a few days to transform her into Annabel." She bent to open the silver box she carried with her.

"In the meantime, I have work to do," I said, turning to leave.

Looking over my shoulder, I caught Mordred's eyes. I could feel the adrenaline running through him, and my blood responded accordingly. Nodding my head ever so slightly, I beckoned for him to follow me.

DAY 31

Over the next couple of weeks, Mordred and I made our way through the country, recruiting men and women to our cause and sending them to Avalon. It was much easier to persuade the masses than I expected. Apparently spending a lifetime hiding who they were, didn't appeal to the majority of the Magical community. Shocking.

Those who were discarded and driven to the margins of society welcomed me with open arms. It was with them I felt the world fall onto my shoulders. This time I wouldn't be so arrogant, this time I'd keep my guard up with a watchful eye on even the most loyal.

I had Vivian to thank for my new found patience and paranoia. If she hadn't dragged me beyond The Veil to spend centuries playing my mistakes over and over in my head, I might not be so prepared to reclaim my throne.

"You ready?" Mordred asked. Concern welled up inside him as his eyes scrutinized my pensive and quiet demeanor.

I cleared my throat, tossing aside any notion of Vivian. "I was born ready."

He held out his hand for me to take and guided me into the circle of his arms.

"Show 'em what you're made of." His voice was low and husky as he pressed his lips to mine.

A yearning to take him right here and now stirred in my abdomen, and I pressed myself against his chest. In the last few weeks, the barriers between Mordred and I had fallen away. Without prying eyes, we were able to rediscover each other in mind and body. Though centuries had passed, we learned that some things never changed.

Regretfully untangling myself from him, I said, "I always do."

The blood in my veins sang, and my heart accelerated as I walked toward the recruits Mordred had sourced for me. This is what I lived for, talking to my people, the Magical ones left behind without a voice. The ones I could show a better life to, the ones who needed someone to stand up and fight for them; these were my people, the people of Le Fay. I'll have them eating out of my palm in the blink of an eye.

Stepping up onto a dusty, metal workbench, I raised myself above the throng of spectators. Removing the bracelet that Mordred gave me to block a Soothsayer's vision, I slipped the delicate bangle into my pocket, making certain that its power wouldn't stop Violet from seeing this.

"Good evening," I said loud enough for those in the back to hear my words.

The sound of work boots shuffling on the gravel as they drew closer was reminiscent of my previous army following me through the gates of Camelot.

"The time has come to embrace who we are and flee from the shadows." There were a few faces in the crowd who looked up at me expectantly, hope glazing their puffy, tired eyes. Others seemed annoyed at the interruption.

"No longer will we hide our Magic. No longer will we fear who we are," I continued.

A few people clapped as concerned grumbles made waves through the crowd.

"You sir," I said, pointing with one long finger toward a gentleman in a black shirt and jeans. There was a passion to him, a hunger that matched my own as I took in his dirt-stained clothing.

He looked from side to side, a nervous energy vibrating off of him as he pointed at his chest and looked up to meet my eyes.

"Yes, you." I stepped down from my perch and walked toward him. With each step, I could feel the thrill of excitement jumping through him like a flea on a dog as I moved through the throng of people.

The crowd parted like the sea as I moved through them, and they formed a circle around me and the gentleman I sought. "Tell me your name?" I planted a finger on his chest and traced a design down his torso that was meant to measure his strength and obedience.

"Anthony," he stammered.

"Anthony, aren't you tired of working so hard with your hands when you could use Magic?" I lifted my head to meet his eyes. The ugly stain of being forced into a life he didn't want, colored his features.

Anthony licked his lips and said, "Yeah, I mean, I guess so." He shrugged and rubbed the back of his neck.

"Then what's stopping you?" The words fell off of my tongue like a kitten purring, and I pushed myself a little closer to him.

His Adam's apple bobbed up and down. "Well, umm." He looked from side to side. "It's forbidden."

Shaking my head, I stepped away from him and said, "Oh, and are you a good little pet? Always playing by the rules?" I batted my lashes like a young girl trying to charm a boy.

"I'm no one's pet," Anthony growled and puffed out his chest like a proud pigeon.

Men are so easy, I thought.

"Then prove it. Show everyone you're not afraid to be who you are." I rushed back to him in a few short steps, the ferocity back in my voice. "Show them you'll no longer play their little game of hide and seek."

I could feel the souls around me twisting and bending to my will. I could feel it in their bones. They wanted this, they yearned to be free.

One man yelled out, "Show 'em Tony!" and started cheering. Another threw his fist in the air and said, "You ain't no pet!" And then they all applauded.

Standing in the midst of the crowd, I crossed my arms as a deadly grin stretched across my lips. They were mine with just a few short words.

I cleared my throat, and my new followers simmered down and waited with bated breath for me to speak again.

I turned my back on Anthony and looked to the others in the crowd, catching the eyes of each person standing before me.

"Will you not fight to free the Magical world?" I spoke each word with a passion that would ignite a hunger for justice in even the most reluctant person.

A thunderous roar erupted from the men surrounding me.

"Who among you will step forward," I asked as I swung my arms open wide, gesturing to all of them, "and claim their place in history?"

Anthony stepped forward. "I will," he said, with a ferocious growl.

I leveled my eyes at him and pursed my lips as I thought, *Of course you will, my pet.*

Pulling a crude dagger from the inside of my boot, I pressed the tip of the blade against my index finger and stepped toward him.

"Take off your shirt." I bit my lip, and a breeze rustled my hair as I looked him up and down. He was the perfect candidate to bear the mark of Le Fay, and I knew without a doubt he would serve me well.

Anthony lifted his shirt over his head, revealing a muscular torso. Wadding the fabric into a ball, he threw it into the dirt. My eyes danced up the length of his bare torso.

Pressing the tip of the dagger near his collarbone, I dug in and branded him as mine. Only a handful could wear my mark proudly, and all would envy those whom I'd chosen.

Anthony's jaw clenched, but he kept his gaze glued to something off in the distance. Not once did he make a sound as blood dripped down his chest and collected at the hem of his trousers.

Placing the palm of my hand against the bloody wound, I recited the spell, *"Hoc est corpus."*

The sound of skin sizzling filled the air as I continued, *"Et ad sanguinem."* My voice rose with each word as I finished the incantation and removed my hand from his chest.

Where a fresh wound had been moments ago, now just an angry red scar remained.

"Who's next?" I asked, looking around the circle. Every one of them stepped forward as a wave of unbridled loyalty washed over me.

They were mine, every last one of them.

I looked off in the distance and smiled. I wanted the last image in Violet's head to be of me amassing an army she could never defeat.

Pulling the bracelet from my pocket, I slipped it back onto my wrist and felt the Magical barrier fall over me like a veil. That would be quite enough to spur Violet into action without her any wiser to our plans.

Branding the few to lead the many, I made the rest bend a knee and take the oath of Le Fay. With their words bound to my will, we were one step closer to restoring my throne and returning Nimue to her family.

"You've caused quite a stir," Mordred said under his breath

as he sidled up next to me. Firelight danced across his face as he kept his eyes on the recruits.

"Yes well, I always did know how to reach the hearts of men."

His head turned, one eyebrow cocked as his eyes met mine. "From what I recall, it wasn't just their hearts-"

"Mordred," I cut him off and smacked his chest playfully.

He chuckled and turned his attention back to the men celebrating their newfound loyalty.

"The short, blonde fellow on the left side," Mordred spoke softly. "The quiet one."

"What of him?" I easily picked out the gentleman in question.

"He claims to have information on the whereabouts of Excalibur."

My heart stuttered in my chest as I studied the frail man in front of me. He was unassuming as he sat and watched the others laughing and sharing stories. On the surface, he was one of them; cast aside, forgotten and forced into a life without Magic. But deep down he was different, I could feel it in him. His colleagues must have picked up on his otherness as well, since they all kept a respectful distance.

"You don't believe him?" I asked, as the outcast took a sip of his beverage and scratched the stubble on his cheek.

"It seems a bit too convenient."

Summoning my Magic, I reached out to him, hoping to get a better sense of who he was and what he was about. His emotions were clouded and fleeting, but there was a familiarity to him, something I've felt before.

"Bring him to me," I said. "Either way, he needs to be dealt with."

As Mordred motioned for the gentleman to approach us, the haze of who he was fell away.

"Hello, Keeper," I said as he came to a stop in front of me.

"Morgana." He inclined his head once and a few strands of his blonde hair fell in front of his eyes.

"Allow us a moment, Mordred."

"Do you think that wise?" he asked under his breath.

"Quite. This gentleman and I must discuss something privately."

"I won't be far," he whispered.

"It's been a long time since I've had the pleasure of meeting one of your kind."

"I must say, it's delightful to see the stories about you are all true." He turned to look at the souls I turned in my favor.

"What is it I can do for you, Keeper?"

"We know you covet someone beyond this realm, and I must warn you to tread lightly."

"I didn't realize the brotherhood would see fit to threaten me?" I eyed him.

"Her soul belongs to the Shadowlands," he said matter-of-factly.

"Nimue's soul belongs to the Shadowlands, yes, but no realm is keeper of The Lady of The Lake."

"Clever girl," he mused. "While this is true, I must still warn you. Reaching beyond this realm will cost you more than you may be willing to pay."

"Nimue deserves to be free."

"That may be true, but she made a deal with the Shadowlands, and a bargain with that realm isn't easily broken."

"That much I know." I shifted my weight. So far he hasn't told me anything I didn't already know. "What is it that brought you here?" I asked.

"My elders do not condone what you've set out to do. But I do, there's a fire in you I admire and I believe you and Nimue will do great things. I offer you my council, one question, which I will answer."

"Mordred said you knew something about the whereabouts of Excalibur."

"I do." A crooked smile played on his lips.

"Tell me where it is, Keeper."

"Not where, but with who. Find Michael Ainsworth, and you'll find your sword."

"Thank you."

"Be sure you're willing to pay the price when the bill comes due." He bowed his head and walked off into the night.

Mordred sidled up to me. "What was that about?"

"Michael Ainsworth."

"What about him?"

"Find him, and we find Excalibur." I turned to face him.

Mordred looked between the Keeper and me, his eyes crinkling at the corner.

"You trust that man?"

"I do. For he is a Keeper of the Realms."

Mordred's eyes widened, and his head snapped back toward the Keeper who had vanished into thin air.

DAY 35

"We have but one goal today," I addressed the small group of soldiers we brought with us. "Find Excalibur, no matter the cost."

Mordred stepped forward with a frail-looking woman clutching onto his arm.

"Tell her what you told me," Mordred pushed the woman forward, and she fell to her knees in front of me.

"The Ainsworth's keep the sword in their private collection." Her eyes darted between me and the floor.

"And?" I stared down at her.

"One of the smaller houses on the property, Casa del Monte." Her eyes met mine, and her bottom lip fell open. "There's a hidden arms room beneath the structure, that's where they keep it."

"You know this how?" I eyed her.

"I'm employed by the Ainsworth family and tasked with seeing after the bungalows on the south side of the property."

"If you work for them, why give up their secret to us?"

"You'll kill everyone in there to find the sword, will you not?"

67

"Someone knows their history," I smirked.

"If you know where to find the sword, maybe people don't have to die."

"Or maybe this is an elaborate attempt to stall us." I grabbed her face with one hand, and each vein came to life under her pale skin.

"I swear," she said through squished lips. "I only want to spare as many lives as possible." The rush of sincerity pouring out of her was enough to make me believe her as the veins in her neck protruded from her skin.

"Very well." I tightened my grip and allowed my Magic to take hold of her. "Thank you for your honesty."

The whites of her eyes brightened as if the sun was inside her skull. The blood under her skin sizzled across her face and down her neck as chunks of her flesh turned to ash and fluttered to the ground. As the spell took hold of the rest of her body, I released the woman and she disintegrated into nothing but bone.

She was a truthful woman, but a fool to come to me and expect to live beyond our interaction.

"Now that's taken care of," I sighed and stepped around the pile of bones. "They won't expect me to be here on the ground, working alongside you. Mordred and I will put on a show and keep them distracted while you lot look for the sword."

Each of them nodded along to my words.

"You've proven yourself worthy of the task ahead," I addressed our party. "But don't fool yourselves into thinking this will be easy. At the moment we have the upper hand, but it won't last long, and you must never underestimate your enemies. Excalibur has been protected and hidden from me since the day my brother wrapped his grubby little fingers around the hilt, but today that will change."

"Alright then, everyone has their marching orders," Mordred's voice was commanding. "Don't forget to signal the retreat once it's in your possession." He glared after each of them as they turned to fetch what was rightfully mine.

"One last thing," I called. "Cross me, and you'll find the devil himself to be a blessing once I've had my way with you." My lips formed a hard line and my eyes narrowed.

Several of their eyes widened, and a few Adam's apples bobbed up and down.

"Quit gawking and fetch me, my sword."

"Was that necessary?" Mordred shook his head and let out a chuckle as our group dispersed.

"It's always necessary." I placed my hand on his arm. "Shall we?"

Making our way in the opposite direction of my merry band of misfits, Mordred and I sauntered up to the front of the castle without a second glance.

We walked up to the entrance and two men in uniform stepped in front of us. "Ticket?"

I glanced at Mordred, then glanced back at the guards with a grin on my face. Summoning my Magic, tendrils of liquid fire licked across the small space between us and wrapped around the men guarding the entrance. Their bodies smoked as a few people standing by screamed out in terror.

"That should get their attention," Mordred smirked. As we continue to move past them, their bodies crumpled and smoldered into an unrecognizable pile of clothing and flesh.

One woman ran past me, holding her child in her arms and shielding the babe's face from my view. Her eyes caught mine for a brief moment and I felt the sheer terror of the woman's heart palpitate around her. I let my gaze pass over her and focused on the people running toward us like rats trying to escape to safety.

Amongst those running in terror, I could spot the few brave souls running toward the fight. That was, of course, until they spotted me. Each of them froze as their eyes took me in.

Magical shields popped into existence the moment their brain registered that the commotion wasn't some mere accident, but instead an act of war.

Summoning devil's flame, I threw out both of my arms and let the fire dance around us as it searched for its victim. Mordred knelt next to me, placing one hand on the concrete. The ground beneath us shook, and a low rumble built all around us as Mordred's Magic burrowed into the earth, and took root in the foundation of the castle. Bolts of electricity and cinder orbs flew in our direction, and I deflected each spell with ease.

This is child's play, I thought.

I raised my arms above my head, forming a ball of fire the size of a large boulder, and hurled it toward a large crowd trying to escape from the nearest building. One of the women battling against us let her shield drop and refocused it on the would-be victims of the blazing sphere, which bounced off of her force field and crashed into the building behind the crowd. Stone flew in every direction and fire rained down on the surrounding area. As the woman let out a sigh of relief that everyone was left unscathed, the Devil's flame found a home by sinking its talons into her skin and burning her from the inside out. She fell to her knees in front of me and screamed as the flames devoured her like a rabid pack of animals.

As she succumbed to her fate, someone else shot off a Warning spell which exploded like a cannon above our heads. Within seconds three more people ran toward the battle, shields raised as they took in the destruction around them.

"Time to dance," Mordred said under his breath and ran toward the closest person. Green sparks flickered on the tips of his fingers, and his knuckles connected with the shield, and both parties fell backward.

Turning my attention to the others, I paced in front of the crumpled body at my feet.

"You can't take all of us," a tall, well-built man yelled.

"Can't I though?" I frowned.

With little effort, I drew on the electric current running through the air and released a bolt of electricity that sent them all flying backward.

Pushing forward, Disarming spells and Cinder orbs assaulted me, but none could penetrate my shield. I moved toward the man who threatened me and lifted him to his feet with a flick of my finger. He held his shield steady, but that wouldn't be a problem. Leaning as close as I dared, I whispered, "What was it you were saying?"

His eyes widened, and I reached through his shield, placed my hand on his chest and let a raw burst of Magic erupt inside his heart. I release my hold on him, and he fell to the ground like a sack of potatoes.

Mordred pulled up next to me and kicked at the body lying at my feet.

"We need to keep moving."

"One last thing." I turned to face the few who remained standing. Holding my palms open to the sky, blue flames rushed toward the three still stupid enough to try to fight me. They linked arms, and a sphere took shape around them, cracking along the surface like ice and forming a barrier between them and me.

My flames hit their wall, a deafening *boom* bouncing off every surface and rattling my bones. Ears ringing, I held the spell steady. They may be stronger together, but their strength was still no match for mine.

Piece by piece, their shield fell away in chunks, allowing the flames to taste their skin. My Magic sprung into a fury as tendrils of the blue flame wrapped around their bodies like snakes. There was no escape now, even if they could manage to keep their shield up. The rope-like flames curled around the middle of each of them, crushing their torsos in an unbreakable grip. As the spell lifted them from their feet, they squirmed, allowing the Magic to feed off of their panic. One attempted a Disarming spell, but it was too late. The more they fought, the stronger the spell became. This Magic has always been my specialty: Making their last efforts to survive work against them.

Nimue's words echoed in my head, *The strongest instinct in a human is to survive. If you can use that against them, they will be no match for you.*

"Morgana, enough play, we have to keep moving," Mordred yelled over the roar of my Magic.

As much as I was enjoying myself, he was right. Grabbing onto the flames bursting from my palms, I yanked hard once and their bodies fell limp. My Magic retracted into me, leaving their dead bodies to join the others now littering the entryway.

Turning to face Mordred, a smile pulled at his lips.

"Shall we?"

A chuckle escaped his throat, and he turned to run up the second set of stairs to our right. As I followed behind him, people ran in every direction screaming and crying. A large group stood in our way, just a few feet ahead of us. One man was giving orders as others crowded around a pile of rubble, trying to lift a large chunk of building off of a bloody and broken figure.

"Inpulsa." A shock wave ran through the group, tossing them in every direction and clearing the way for us to pass.

As we rounded the corner, the sounds of battle fell behind us. Crisp blue water contrasted with white stone and marble stretched as far as the eye could see.

"Stop this!" A deep, raspy voice yelled from behind us.

I turned to face the man who'd spoken and said, "Bring me what I seek, and we'll leave without killing anyone else."

Motioning for Mordred and Anthony to watch out for

others, I flicked my wrist once, and the man in front of me dropped to his knees.

"I won't let you have it," he yelled as blood trailed down the side of his face and neck.

"No one tells me what I can and can't have," I said through gritted teeth. Curling my fist into a ball, I pulled him toward me, his knees dragging across the cement floor.

"No matter the cost, we will keep Excalibur under our protection, Morgana." He used my name like a curse.

"It would appear that I'm at a disadvantage," I said, grabbing his jaw and looking into his amber eyes. "You know my name, but alas, you have not told me yours." A mixture of ragged fear and acceptance wafted off of him like a rotting corpse. I fought the urge to recoil and looked deeper into his soul.

A whisper on the breeze made my ears perk up. A voice that had long since eluded me gave me the name I sought.

"Does it matter? You'll kill me either way," he snarled.

"Not necessarily." I released his face and knelt down so we were eye to eye. "Tell me where to find Excalibur, and I'll let you live, Michael Ainsworth."

A thrill ran through me as terror flashed across his eyes at the sound of his name. Many knew of my power, but it wasn't until they experienced it up close and personal that they realized just how limitless my Magic is.

"You're an abomination," he spat.

"And here I thought we were making friends," I pouted and shrugged.

Turning to face the massive pool lying twenty feet away, I lifted my hand, forcing Michael to rise to his feet and walk into the shallow water.

"Drowning is a terrible way to die. Your lungs burning, struggling for one last taste of oxygen, knowing life is within reach and not being able to grasp it," I let the acid in my words drip off my tongue.

Michael looked around, searching for salvation when I slammed my hand toward the ground, and he fell to his knees.

"Last chance." I leveled my eyes at him, willing him to tell me where the sword was.

"Do what you will," he said and closed his eyes. To the others he looked brave, fighting to keep the sword a secret until his death, but I could feel the true tenor of his soul. Terror gripped his heart as he held onto his last shred of hope. He wasn't brave; he was a coward.

"Very well." Disgust rose inside me as I lifted my hands above my head. Water formed into a sphere around him, encasing him in a watery tomb. There was no escaping. The orb of crystal clear water swirled around him, spinning on an axis much like the earth at neck-breaking speeds and throwing him end over end. At first, he didn't struggle, determined not to let his true will to survive show, but as the seconds ticked by, he fought back. His arms and legs pushed against the water as if he was swimming against Titan's current to no avail. With his physical abilities proving useless, he turned to Magic, conjuring spell after spell, but I thwarted him each time, keeping him wrapped in his aquatic grave.

"Let him go," a woman shrieked over the roar of the water, sucking the life out of Michael.

Turning to see who dared challenge me, my eyes skipped over the tiny woman and landed on the sword in her hand.

"Excalibur," I said under my breath as she pointed the blade directly at me.

The liquid sphere holding Michael shattered as I released my hold on him. The sharp sting of water against the ground and Michael's gasp for air reached my ears as I stepped toward my prize.

"I'll give you credit; you're a brave little thing." I smiled and let the tip of the blade press into my chest. "But I'll be returning this to its rightful owner."

"This sword belongs to none other than King Arthur. If you want it, you'll have to pry it from my cold, dead hands."

I clicked my tongue in disapproval. "Do you believe anyone can stop me from taking what I want?"

"Leave Morgana. You're outnumbered." Her voice wavered, but her sword arm straightened a little tighter, and I could feel the blade prick my skin, sending a warm droplet of blood down my chest.

Finally, someone who wasn't afraid to play dirty.

"Ariana," Michael called from behind me, his emotions hitting me like a brick wall. Love and fear were coalescing into an almost overwhelming geyser of sentiment. "Don't," he choked out.

Her eyes caught his, and her stoic guard fell for the briefest of moments. She cared for him just as much as he did for her. Had they been smart, they wouldn't have shown their weakness in front of me.

Taking a step backward, I summoned the Magic aching within me and lifted Michael from his knees once more. Pulling him effortlessly through the air, I brought him to his knees in front of me, making sure he was facing her. With a flick of my wrist, a cinder orb appeared in my palm, spinning and dancing to an unheard cadence.

"You have a choice, Ariana." I placed my hand on Michael's shoulder, and I felt her pain echo in his heart. "The sword for Michael's life."

Her mouth fell open, and the tip of the sword dipped ever so slightly.

As if on cue, a deep rumble vibrated the ground as an explosion from somewhere within rocked the foundation.

"I'm not known for my patience, Ariana," I said through gritted teeth.

"You'll leave, all of you?" Her voice quivered.

"Of course." I did my best to keep my face neutral.

A man jumped out of the hedges to my right and yelled, "If you won't finish her-"

The cinder orb in my palm found its home, cutting off any further interruption, turning the intruder to dust before our eyes.

"I'm not here to play games." I summoned another orb. "Give me the sword now, or I will kill your beloved." The poison in my voice was unmistakable.

Ariana dropped the sword, the metal clanking off the cement as it came to a rest at her feet.

I let the cinder orb dissipate and said, "Grab her." Yellow vines erupted from Mordred and bound Ariana as our prisoner.

"Wait. No! You said you'd let us go?" Michael scrambled to his feet as I plucked the sword from the ground, feeling the cool steel settle against my palm.

"I believe I said I wouldn't kill you," My eyes traced the edge of the blade.

"Please, Morgana. You have what you want," he pleaded.

"Indeed, I do." Another explosion sounded within the castle and sirens screamed in the distance. "And I believe that's our cue."

Mordred nodded once and threw Ariana over his shoulder.

"You can't do this," Michael screamed, and a bolt of lightning shot toward me. Swinging the sword up in front of me, the spell bounced off the metal and hit a sculpture to my left. Bits and pieces of marble erupted around us as a statue of a Goddess exploded into a million pieces.

Waving my hand over my head, a wall of fire encircled Michael. A feral scream tore through him, and a spell broke through the fire hurling toward me. Before I could lift a finger to disarm the spell, Anthony stepped in front of me and deflected the orb with little effort.

"I'll take care of him," Anthony said over his shoulder.

"Leave him alive, just barely," I said.

"Your Grace?" Anthony's brow furrowed and flames roared behind him.

"Death is easy," I remarked. "Feeling the gut-wrenching loss of someone he loves, that'll teach him not to trifle in matters bigger than himself.

Anthony smirked and turned to face Michael.

"Don't let anyone say I don't keep my promises," I said, meeting Mordred's eyes.

"I'm sure he'll regret the gift of life you're granting him," Mordred said, adjusting Ariana's weight on his shoulder.

As we disappeared behind a wall of smoke, the sound of rocks exploding behind us overwhelmed every other sense.

Following Mordred through the carnage, the sword firmly in my grip, I let myself relish the moment. Arthur had spent his last breath trying to keep Excalibur from me. Now, after what seemed like an eternity, it was mine.

With the castle behind us, I paused to take one last look. Despair, confusion, and anger cried out and touched me, as the losing side took stock of what was left. Let this be a lesson to them all. I was back with a vengeance and no one, not even The Waker, could stop me.

DAY 36

When we arrived at the rendezvous point, Mordred split off to secure the prisoner while I made my way through the house and into the furthest bedroom. Placing Excalibur in the washing basin, I turned on the water and submerged the blade.

"*Revelare*," I said over the sword. Etchings hidden under the surface now sizzled brightly on the steel. Steam filled the small room as the heat of the blade drew upon the water as a source of power. I lifted the sword from the basin and ran my finger against the chiseled words. They were hot to the touch, just as they would have been when they were forged into the molten steel.

Vivian was wise to leave behind breadcrumbs that would allow her to return from beyond The Veil. Unfortunately for her, they would also help me save Nimue and put an end to Vivian once and for all.

"*Iungo nostrum mundos*," I began. The edges of the sword lit up a brilliant orange as the enchantment permeated Excalibur. I opened the vial of Mordred's blood and dipped my finger in the crimson liquid. Running his blood along the edge of the sword, it smoldered and turned a brownish black color until the blade absorbed every last drop.

"*Proucat terra obumbratio*," I completed the enchantment that would call upon the Shadowlands when the time came.

I may not be able to alter Merlin's spell, but I could transform the purpose of the sword. Once Violet fulfills her destiny, the enchantment will activate and reach out to Nimue, the true Lady of The Lake.

With the enchantment in place, I wrapped the blade in a blanket and recited a Cloaking spell to keep it safe.

Exhaustion seeped into my bones as the desire to rest pulled at every muscle in my body. I sat on the corner of the bed and fell backward, replaying today's victory. It would be unthinkable for anyone to dispute my strength or position within the Magical world now.

Tap, Tap, Tap.

"It's me." Mordred's muffled voice came through the door.

"Come in."

"I've got good news and bad news," he said.

"Always the bad news first, Mordred," I sighed.

"Everything alright?"

"Of course," I sat up. "Just taking a quiet moment to myself. So, bad news?"

"We have to postpone our trip back to Avalon." He closed the door behind him.

"Oh?"

He smirked. "We've placed another one of Vivian's tokens."

"So soon?"

"We've been searching for the tokens for a while now, and information has come to light on the heels of our victory."

"It would serve you well to be cautious of those who willingly offer such delicious information at a time like this." I stood and closed the space between us.

"I know better than to trust any ol' fool with gossip." He

pushed the hair off of my shoulder, and his hand rested on my waist. "I've vetted the information on various fronts."

"Very well, which token do we hunt this time?"

"The Lufian Necklace."

"That blasted thing. I never could understand her fascination with turning one's desires against them."

"Vivian's a monster, incapable of understanding anything other than her own twisted form of justice."

"Indeed." I placed my hand on his chest, the memory of Vivian's justice still fresh in my heart. "Where, pray tell, is her necklace?"

"There's a tiny hiccup with its location."

"Nothing worth having comes easy," I said.

His arms slithered around me. "We know the necklace will be delivered to Huntington Library, but not when."

"That does pose a problem." I wrapped my arms around his neck. "We very well can't wait around, hoping for it to show up."

"A queen waits for no one," he whispered against my lips. "We've tracked the man who's arranging the delivery. He's one of theirs, but I think we can break him." His lips touched mine, and the electric shock that ran through me banished the weariness in my bones.

"Won't that be fun," I smirked as my fingers laced through his hair and I pushed the length of my body against his.

Voices boomed from the front of the house, accompanied by a raucous round of cheers, reminding us we weren't alone. No doubt they were celebrating our victory. A victory I was keen to celebrate too, I thought, as I bit his bottom lip.

"The sword?" He whispered.

"Safe for now." I pulled his shirt over his head.

My eyes devoured him as I tossed the wad of fabric to the floor. I delighted in feeling the fire in his veins match my own inferno as we latched onto one another.

"How long until they know?" He asked as his lips moved down my neck.

I let out a heavy breath. "If Violet doesn't know already, she will soon."

His teeth grazed the delicate skin at my throat as he pushed me against the closed door. Closing my eyes, I melted into his capable hands as his lips found mine.

"We should expect them to retaliate." His voice was husky as he broke our kiss.

"I would expect nothing less." I dug my nails into his shoulders as his hands traced the curve of my back and settled on my hips. "She needs to be ready," I breathed. "Or all of this will be for nothing."

His body pressed against mine and I could feel his heart hammering in his chest. Tracing my collarbone with his lips, his breath hot on my skin.

"We'll make sure of it," he said, sending a shiver through my abdomen like lightning.

The sound of fire crackling from somewhere within the room diverted my attention from the man in front of me. Looking over Mordred's shoulder, a blue and orange flaming bird fluttered in the air.

Mordred's head fell against mine. "Another fire message?" He sighed.

I could hear the frustration in his voice, but we both understood that our time together was not our own. At least not yet. Once we freed the Magical world and reclaimed my rightful place, we'd have all the time in the world.

"You know there are easier ways to communicate nowadays." He shook his head.

"Yes, but Magic is reliable and natural, unlike your gadgets." I placed my hands on his biceps. "Have you forgotten what is natural will always be superior to anything derived from the narrow minds of men."

"Maybe I need you to remind me." His lips fell on mine again as he pinned me between his body and the door.

I pulled away from his kiss. "I'd be happy to jog your memory." I let my hand linger down his chest, fighting the urge to give into his pleading gaze. "But right now, I must attend to business," I said, freeing myself from his arms.

"Don't think I won't hold you to that." He bent to pick up his discarded shirt.

"I know you will," I purred as the swallow landed on my open palm.

"The sweetness of love is short-lived," the bird's velvet voice cooed from its perch.

"But the pain endures," I replied.

Like a dandelion on a gentle breeze, the facade of the bird blew away to reveal a folded piece of paper.

I unfolded the letter and read as Mordred wrestled into his shirt.

"Who's it from," he asked.

"Alyssa," I said without looking up. "It would seem that it's time for Annabel to rejoin her family."

Mordred plucked Alyssa's words from my hand. His eyes devoured their meaning, and his mouth fell open as he reached the small picture of Emilia with Annabel's face.

"The likeness is uncanny, but are you sure she's ready?"

"Alyssa assures me Emilia will look, act and recall memories just as Annabel would. She also mentioned it's been a breeze extracting memories from the girl in her weak state."

"Alyssa has outdone herself this time." His voice was soft, but the tenor of his heart was uneasy. For some reason, Mordred was hesitant to believe in this plan.

"What is it?" I asked as he handed me the letter.

He let out a heavy sigh. "I still worry about the amount of trust you're putting in Emilia." He turned to face me. "Her history with Lila complicates things."

"As does your history with Lila," I shot back. "It's a tangled web Aiden's daughter has spun, but I believe Emilia can handle it."

Mordred may not believe in her, but he also didn't know the nature of Emilia's heart the way I did. Lila may have been an issue for her in the past, but she no longer clouded her present as it did with him.

"I defer to your judgment, of course, I just don't want to see you get hurt again." His eyes fell away from mine and a century of heartache swam around us.

"This isn't like last time." I placed my hand on his shoulder.

"You see yourself in her, don't you?"

"She's an asset, that's all."

"An asset that you're willing to send to the wolves." He ran a hand through his hair. "An asset who earned your trust in a matter of days. An asset who has ties to someone who betrayed me. Us."

"Is that what this is about? You think she'll turn like your Lila did?"

"I can't rule it out, and it scares the shit out of me to think I could lose you again."

"I'm not going anywhere. Not this time." The sharpness in my voice made my words final.

Mordred grabbed my hands. "I know, but you can't fault me for worrying about you."

"Worrying will be the death of you." I gave his hands a gentle squeeze.

"Death is a friend I'll never meet, remember." A short, humorless laugh escaped his throat.

"There's more than one way to die," I noted.

Silence fell between us as I pulled away from him and sat down to reply to Alyssa's letter.

Mordred cleared his throat. "We'll need to leave within the

hour if we want to stay ahead of Violet and the others. I should ready the troops."

"The devastation at the castle will've bought us some time," I replied. "They'll want to tend to the victims before they chase after us." I pulled a piece of paper from the desk and began to write.

"Still, they won't be far behind us. The Maxwells are quick to regroup and retaliate. We should be swift about leaving here."

"You didn't say, where exactly is Huntington Library?" I asked, looking up at him.

"Los Angeles." He pulled a piece of paper from his pocket. "The coordinates to the informant."

"Thank you," I said, brushing my fingers against his as I took the note from him. "For everything."

Mordred dropped to his knee in front of me, still holding my hand. "You never have to thank me for-"

"I want to." I placed my hands on either side of his face. "I wouldn't be here without you, and I know your concern comes from a good place." I placed my lips on his and whispered, "So thank you."

"Always, my Queen." He gave my hand a gentle squeeze and stood. "How long will the portal take you?" Our moment of vulnerability vanished, and he was back to business. It's what I always loved about him. He was practical and understood that some things were bigger than him and me.

"Not long at all."

I added the coordinates Mordred had given me to the bottom of the letter and signed the note with the symbol of Le Fay.

"*Nuntius Ignis. Emilia.*" The letter erupted in blue flames. Bits of ash and sparks danced in the air, swirling around me and then vanishing in a puff of smoke.

"Ready my knights," I smirked.

Mordred left without another word, closing the door

behind him.

I stepped up to the sliding glass door and smiled at my reflection. "Los Angeles, here we come."

Pulling the dagger from my boot, I cut open my palm, allowing blood to pool and drip between my fingers. Portal Magic was never easy, and many have paid the price with their life to cross time and space.

I dipped my index finger in my blood and drew four circles on the glass, which represented not only the elements, but the four corners of a compass. Filling in the details for each circle, I drew the fifth and final elemental circle for Magic in the middle of the compass.

"Iter per tempus," I recited the spell to open the portal while drawing a diamond shape to enclose the elemental circles. Immediately, I felt my heart falter as the spell devoured my Magic.

"Ad locum meum eligendo." My ears rang, and the blood on my palm flowed more freely.

The circles hovered off of the glass, moving toward me, seeking the location of my desire as my knees buckled. The amount of Magic pouring out of me would leave me dead if I didn't hurry to complete the spell.

Dabbing my finger in my blood once more, my hand shook as I marked the glass inside the diamond shape with the coordinates Mordred had given me. Falling to my knees, I reached up, placed my palm against the shimmering Magic element and finished the spell, *"nunc aperire."*

The diamond shape shimmered as the north and south elements spun clockwise, and the east and west elements spun counter clockwise. The Magical element beneath my palm slammed against the glass, shattering it as it pulled energy from the elements instead of me. Letting out a heavy sigh, I struggled to get to my feet as the portal that would take us to the next token began to take shape.

DAY 40

After the library closed, we set up inside a large storage room with a few dozen soldiers. I could handle this with half that amount, but we had to keep up appearances. As long as Violet was worried about us trying to stop her, she wouldn't be tempted to look at our motives and Emilia could slip among their ranks without question.

I looked over the room with careful eyes. A scruffy, average built man stood at the other end of the room, his eyes trained on the floor and orb bouncing in his hand. Hushed conversations moved through the room like ghosts as they waited for the curtain to rise on tonight's little drama.

Emilia stood away from everyone, starting the process of her transformation as Mordred sidled up to her. He rolled his stiff shoulders, and his eyes stayed glued to the bottles on the table.

"That's quite a collection you've got there," he said, picking up one of the bottles.

"It's a complicated spell." She took the vial he was holding and replaced it on the table.

"You're sure you're ready for this?" he asked her.

"More than ready," she fired back. The corner of my lips

turned up at the pride in her voice. She was an ideal choice for this mission.

"And Lila?" He asked under his breath, and I could sense the shame roll off him as he said her name.

Emilia looked up at him. "She's nothing but the past."

"You say that now, but will it be so easy to turn a blind eye once you're with them?"

Emilia mumbled a spell under her breath and swallowed the first of several doses that would allow her to keep up appearances.

"Mordred, leave Emilia to prepare." I motioned him over to me.

Emilia reached out and grabbed Mordred's arm before he could turn to leave. "I understand your concern. I do. But my loyalty lies with Morgana. Of that much, you can trust."

"I just-"

"Have something to lose," she interrupted.

He nodded and sauntered toward me. His lips stretching into a tight grin as shame curled around him.

"Why do you still question my judgment?" I lowered my voice so only he could hear my words. It would only undermine our mission here if Mordred and I had it out in front of everyone, but enough was enough. I'd made my decision about Emilia and her usefulness.

He cleared his throat. "I don't."

"Then why do you insist on questioning Emilia's loyalty at every opportunity? Has she done something to you, or offended you in some way?"

"She has a temper that I don't trust." He folded his arms over his chest.

"A temper that we can use. Don't you see that?"

"You can only use and mold the naïve, Morgana. And Emilia is anything but."

I mulled over his words. She was prone to anger and hatred;

it was a quality I recognized in her almost immediately. But she wasn't reckless.

"What you fail to grasp is that I don't have to mold her. I've given her rage and grief an outlet: Fighting for a better Magical world, one where she is accepted for her merits and she can thrive. There's no need to manipulate those who are willing to bend to my will."

"Sure, she has a purpose now, a life free of Aiden's abuse. But have you asked yourself why she was so eager to pledge her allegiance?"

"You've been playing with fire far too long, my dear Mordred. It's made you paranoid."

"All I ask is that you maintain awareness of those around you."

"Your concern is noted," I said, placing my hand on his chest. "Now let it go."

The door to our little hideout creaked open and suppressed any rebuttal from Mordred.

"They're here," Anthony said, stepping into the room, his eyes wide and feverish.

"Time to have a little fun," I smirked. "You know your orders," I said, addressing the room. "Do not harm, Violet, but do what you will with the others."

The men and women who volunteered to join us on this mission filed out of the room to perform the second act of our play.

"Anthony, Mordred, stay behind," I called to them.

"Are you ready?" I asked Emilia as her features morphed into Annabel's.

She was nervous; it didn't take someone with my ability to see that. But as nervous as she was, I could feel the current of determination running through her.

"I'm good." She buttoned a pair of beat up trousers.

The shirt she changed into was the one Annabel wore when

Mordred brought her to Avalon. A nice little detail, I thought. Dirt and blood splattered the fabric, completing the weary prisoner look.

"I will have to hurt you, but I can numb the pain." I placed my hand on her shoulder.

"I know. I can take it, do what you must."

"And their healer won't be able to help you," I reminded her.

"I know." She smirked. "But it's better they learn firsthand how weak they are without their Healer."

"I'll do what I can to keep as much of the pain at bay, but I need you to play it up as best you can."

"Understood," Emilia said in Annabel's delicate voice.

The warehouse shook as if the earth was being split in two and the lights plunged into darkness.

"That's my cue." I gave Emilia a tight-lipped smile and turned to Mordred. "I'll call for you when I'm ready."

I stepped through the door, took one last look at Emilia who was now a stunning image of Annabel, and marched onto the stage.

DAY 41

Not to my surprise, Violet made the exchange for her friend, and Emilia was taken away with the enemy as one of their own. Once the healing properties of the spell I used to torture her took hold, she'd be able to fulfill her part in this little drama.

I held the Lufian necklace between my fingers and recited the spell to call upon the Magic within. Before my eyes, the token crumbled and turned to ash, covering my fingers in gray velvet soot.

Fury, like I haven't known in ages, tore at my skin. My hands shook as my vision became laser-focused on the smooth gray texture coating my palm.

"That clay-brained lout," I shouted and heaved a bolt of raw Magic into the wall across from me. Rubble exploded through the room, leaving a thick haze of smoke and dust hanging in the air.

Mordred rushed into the room, sparks dancing on his fingers. "What happened?" He looked around expectantly.

"Violet," I said through gritted teeth.

"She's here?" Mordred's brow furrowed.

"Of course not," I spat.

The tension in his shoulders eased as his Magic receded into him.

"That swine switched the necklace with a fake."

"The enchantment?"

I shook my head. "As it stands, Excalibur is useless. It won't be strong enough to reach the Shadowlands on its own."

"There's still the ring," he said, but we both understood what it meant if we didn't get to the ring first. We'll have failed, and Nimue would be lost to us forever. "If we can enchant the third token, do you think it will give us enough of a chance?"

"I don't know." I ran my hand through my hair, "And even if it did, we'd still need to get to the ring before they do."

"Then that's what we'll do." Mordred crossed the room and took my hand. "All is not lost. There's still a chance this can work." He dusted the remnants of the fake necklace from my hand.

"When did you become such an optimist?" I rolled my eyes.

The fact that I didn't see this coming left a sour taste in my mouth. I'd underestimated Violet and her little clan, something I wouldn't do again.

"When someone told me anything was possible." He smiled as he repeated my words.

Dunk, dunk, dunk. Three taps on wood pulled my retort from my lips and directed my attention to the hole in the wall.

"Sorry to interrupt," Alyssa stepped through the makeshift door in the wall, her shoes scraping against the debris. "But I think there's something you need to see."

"What is it?" I sighed. I neither had the time or patience to handle yet another issue.

"Annabel, the prisoner. She's acting less than what I'd consider desirable under the conditions."

"And?"

"It has me worried about Emilia."

That caught my attention.

"Has she checked in yet?"

"No," Alyssa's eyes darted between Mordred and me.

"Show me." I motioned for her to take the lead. "And Mordred, have this cleaned up, will you?" I waved my hand at the mess.

I followed Alyssa to the landing and down the stairs. Her steps were quick, and the controlled panic humming around her rattled me. Something was seriously wrong if it was spooking her like this.

"When you say less than desirable?" I asked as we made our way through the front door.

"I've experimented plenty with spells and potions, but I've never seen someone deteriorate this quickly."

Her words were clinical; she kept all emotion out of her voice. I couldn't help but wonder what her motives were for Annabel's well-being.

"Are you worried for the girl or your experiment?"

"They're one and the same, are they not?" She cocked her head as she motioned for me to take the lead into the cellar.

"You can't force the bananas to go on stage." A delicate wind chime voice echoed through the hall.

The cells were almost full now. So many gifted people, unwilling to help those cast aside by our society. It was a shame they refused to join us and rebuild the Magical world for the better. Should they choose not to reconsider, then they'd have no other choice but to forfeit their Magic and live a half-life.

"The candy is poison to the sky," Annabel raised her voice when she spotted us at her cell door.

Leaves and dirt caked her hair as if she'd been sleeping outside. Her pale skin was no longer rosy, but gray and thin, and her eyes were milky, leaving them almost colorless.

"What's happening to her?" I asked.

"Best guess?" Alyssa began, "The spell we used to tap into her memory is messing with her brain."

"Does she know where she is, or who I am?"

"She doesn't seem to have any cognitive faculties left."

"How can you be sure this isn't an act?"

Alyssa unlocked the prison door and stepped inside.

"Annabel, there's someone I'd like you to meet." Alyssa's tone was sickly sweet as she coaxed Annabel out of the corner.

With a shaky hand, Annabel reached out and took hold of Alyssa. Her clothes hung off her body and the sharp bones of her shoulders poked through the tattered fabric.

"This is Morgana, your Queen."

Annabel's eyes widened, and for a moment her milky blue irises focused on me.

"Queen, Queen, and everything green," Annabel said under her breath.

"Annabel," I said as I took her hand in my own.

"Queen, Queen and everything green," she repeated.

The mix of emotions passing through her startled me. Sadness, wonder, pain, and love flittered through her like little birds, too quick to hold on to, but present enough to feel each of them.

I let go of her hand, and Alyssa helped her sit on the small cot inside her cell.

"We need to know if Emilia is displaying similar symptoms." I did little to hide the concern in my voice. Emilia was an asset, one I'd become fond of. After the torture I'd inflicted on her back in Los Angeles, I could only hope she wasn't suffering from Annabel's madness. "I want an update within the hour."

"Yes, of course. I'll have one of the teams check in on her."

Turning on my heel, I swept through the prisoners and out into the fresh air. First the necklace, now this? I couldn't let things spiral out of control. I've come too far to let all of this fall apart now. I looked up at the pale blue twilight sky and I thought of the people I was trying to lead to victory, and of Nimue.

"Nimue," I said under my breath.

I hurried across the lawn toward the cabin. Annabel could die for all I cared, but if this was hurting Emilia and impeding my plans, then I must do what is necessary.

I pushed through the front door and went right to the book-shelf. Nimue had been a skilled medicine woman in my time when the only healer was Merlin, who never saw fit to help those in pain. Except for Arthur, of course.

Running my fingers across the spines of dozens of books, I pulled the small red chronicle from the shelf. I flipped it open to the title page and read, *"Uncommon ales for the less fortunate."*

Closing the book, I made my way back to Alyssa and Annabel. As I marched through the trees, Nimue's book in my hand, I was reminded of a time when she would send me on errands that would take me away from Camelot. Sometimes I'd retrieve a package from another village, other times I would collect ingredients for her spells. I was so young then, so naïve and unaware of the plight that surrounded the Magical world. But even then, Nimue was training me to become the woman I am today.

Stepping into the cellar, I could hear Alyssa's side of a conversation.

"Stay close to Emilia, I want to know if there are any changes," she said.

"She hasn't woken," I stated.

Alyssa put the mobile phone in her pocket and shook her head.

"She has a fever, infections. The Maxwells are doing all they can without Magic. But whatever this is," she pointed to Annabel. "It's affecting Emilia too."

Handing her the book I said, "If there's a way to fix this, it will be in here."

"I'll do what I can," she said, taking the book from my possession.

"Do more than that. Fix this," I growled.

DAY 53

The steady gallop of footsteps on the stairs reached my ears as I waited for Violet. *She was making this too easy,* I thought. Coming here to steal Excalibur from under my nose was a bold move. Lucky for her, it's exactly what I wanted her to do.

Violet, Emilia, who was still wearing Annabel's face, and two others reached the landing, eyes wild and searching for danger as their eyes landed on me.

I cocked my head to the side, watching them scurry like rats down the hall.

"Lila, Go. Morgana's coming," Violet yelled as they slammed the double doors of Aiden's old study closed.

Measuring each step, I sauntered down the hall toward the study. In just a moment they would discover, Excalibur was not in the safe as they imagined, and all hope would be lost until my grand entrance.

"Three, two, one," I said under my breath and a pulse of Magic erupted from me. The double doors swung open and smacked against the walls, startling everyone into silence. I do love a good entrance.

"We meet again," I said.

Without so much as a word, a shield materialized before Violet and Robert unlike any I'd seen in centuries. It was weak, unstable, but I'd recognize it anywhere, *Artognou Magic.*

"And you've learned a few tricks since the last time too," I noted. "You know, I didn't appreciate your little trick with the necklace."

"This can end now, Morgana," Robert barked.

I laughed and leaned against the door frame, crossing my arms.

"You may have learned how to tap into your *Artognou-Magic,* but you still don't have the power to kill me," I smirked.

"It isn't here!" Lila yelled, running out of the wall safe.

"Did you think it would be that easy?" I stepped further into the room.

"Where is it, Morgana?" Violet growled.

"You mean this?" I flicked my wrist and Excalibur appeared out of thin air. "Beautiful, isn't she?" I held the sword by the hilt, turning the blade side to side.

"What do we do?" Violet asked under her breath.

"Arthur never deserved it," I said through gritted teeth. "And neither do you," I spurred her on.

My finger-tips crackled with Magic, begging for a release.

"Back off," Violet barked.

"Do you really think you can stop me?"

"Take another step and find out," she challenged.

I squared my shoulders and straightened my arms at my side, one palm turned up, the other gripping the sword. Taking another step, I threw my arms toward them. The tip of Excalibur pointed at the center of their shield. Hot white electricity struck their defense with such force I was nearly knocked off balance.

"We're leaving here with that sword," Violet vowed.

"Wanna bet?"

"Just keep the shield up," Violet yelled over the roar of my Magic connecting with theirs.

Violet's eyes met mine, her lips moving as she recited a spell. An orb appeared in her hand and she hurled the vile thing at me. Lifting Excalibur in front of me, the orb ricocheted off of the blade, hitting the bookshelf instead and exploding. Books flew into the air, their pages ripped from their binding as fire and smoke took hold of the room.

"Hit her again," Robert grunted.

She summoned the spell again and this time I discarded the sword, as the orb flew through the air, giving them the chance they needed.

"Again," Robert yelled.

The ball of Magic vibrated on her palm as she pitched it at my chest.

Allowing the spell to hit me, I flew across the room until my back hit something solid.

"Lila, the sword," Violet yelled.

Lila darted across the room and reached Excalibur as I got to my feet.

"Hurry," Emilia yelled over the now blazing fire.

"She's right, get out of here," Robert grunted. Sweat was beading off his brow, and he longingly looked at Violet.

"Not without you," she huffed.

"You have to." Lila stepped forward, green sparks flickering on her fingertips. With a nod of her head, she shot the Galvin spell in my direction.

Raising my shield, I easily blocked the spell. There was no need to take a further beating now they had the sword.

"Annabel, get her out of here!" Robert yelled as I squared my shoulder and summoned my Magic.

"What about you two?" Emilia said in Annabel's sweet voice.

"We'll be fine, just get Violet out of here!"

"Robert, no," Violet yelled.

He held her gaze for a fraction of a second, then turned to face me.

"Let's go," Emilia said, pushing the window open.

"Here goes nothing then." Violet threw one leg over the window sill and disappeared. Emilia glanced back at me and then followed Violet to safety.

"While this has been fun, I'm afraid I'm needed elsewhere."

Pure, raw Magic rippled over my body in the space between heartbeats. A shiver ran down my spine as the room stilled for a fraction of a second, and then my Magic burst from my core. Every surface in the room shattered into a million pieces.

Turning on my heel, I left the ruined study without so much as a glance toward Robert and Lila. All that mattered now was getting to Emilia before it was too late.

The groan and creak of trees being ripped apart caught my attention as I made my way through the woods. The battle was still in full force as Violet and her remaining friends fought their way off the island with Excalibur. Little did they know the fight was just another smoke screen so Emilia could bring me the ring and replace it before they noticed it was missing. Once I enchanted the ring, the final act of this little play could begin.

As I reached Nimue's cabin, Emilia came into view. She still wore the prisoner's face, but the tenor of her emotion gave her away the moment I saw her. It was fortunate none of the Maxwells had the ability to sense the nature of another's soul.

"Did anyone see you come here?" I asked as I stepped into the cabin.

"No, they're all too busy with the fight," Emilia said, following behind me and closing the door.

"Hand it over; I'll make this quick."

She pulled the ring from her pocket and held it out gingerly. We both knew what the circular band of metal could do to a soul if allowed access.

Placing the foul thing on the table, I allowed my Magic to

pool on my hands on either side of the ring. Brilliant white light pulsed on my palms, making the ring rattle against the wood. The opaque stone turned blood red as Merlin's spell bubbled to the surface.

"Nimue ego animae meae." The stone lifted from the table and hovered between my open palms, drawing my words into the stone. *"Invocabo te."* I finished the spell, and the ring dropped onto the hardwood surface and wobbled.

I plucked the ring from the table and gingerly handed it back to Emilia.

"Take this, too," I pulled a piece of paper from my pocket.

"What do I have to do?" Her jaw flexed as she read the words scrawled across the paper in her hand.

"Memorize it. Once Violet starts the process of calling upon The Lady of The Lake, you will need to take control of Excalibur and recite that spell."

"How am I supposed to gain access to Excalibur?"

"I'll take care of Violet. Once the rift is open, the rest will be up to you."

Another rumble in the distance caught our attention.

"You should go," I said.

Her mouth fell open as if to say something, but she nodded her head instead.

"You can do this, Emilia," I raised her chin, forcing her to look me in the eyes. "The fate of the Magical world hangs in the balance. Only you can help me tip the scales in our favor."

Her eyes searched mine, and I could feel her resolve melt into place. "I'll send word the moment I know when we're heading out."

"We'll be waiting for you," I said, placing my hand on her shoulder and giving it a gentle squeeze.

Turning on her heel, she was out of sight in a flash.

"Is that it then? They have all the tokens?" Mordred asked from the shadows.

"The stage is set, my dear Mordred." I turned to face him.

He stared at the open door. "In just a few short hours, Nimue may stand before us."

The wood floor creaked as I moved across the cabin to him.

"It's been centuries since I've dared to hope, but you've made the impossible a reality," he said. His hand cupped my cheek, and the soft, inviting grin on his lips warmed my heart. "If I didn't know any better, I'd say you could move mountains with the sheer force of your will."

"If you don't try, then you've already failed," I repeated his mother's words. Nimue drilled into us that there was always a path to victory if you wanted something bad enough.

"I tried for longer than I care to remember, but it was you who found a way."

"Let's hope we've done enough." I looked away.

"You have doubts?" His brow furrowed with concern.

"It bothers me I only enchanted two of the tokens."

"Your Magic is strong-"

"We both know my Magic isn't stronger than Merlin's."

"You can't let what happened, color your perception." His voice was stern.

"This has to work."

"If it doesn't, then we'll try something else," he reassured me.

"Your confidence is unwavering." I rolled my eyes.

"I know who I saved from beyond The Veil." His hand snaked around my waist. "And more than anyone, I know what you're capable of."

The sound of trees being ripped apart rattled my bones and smoke filled the air.

I thought about everything I'd accomplished since my return. Recruiting an army, overthrowing Aiden, enchanting the tokens. This was my time, my world for the taking. I wouldn't let anything get in my way.

DAY 54

The battle was in full force a few hundred feet away. The deep rumble of thunder and the crackle of Magic reached my ears even at this distance. Cloaking myself, I watched as Violet pulled herself over the last boulder and stood atop the large cluster of rocks.

"We made it," Robert exhaled.

Moving toward the altar, she held Excalibur against her palm and sliced open the delicate skin. Blood pooled in her fist and as she held out her hand, pebble-sized drops of blood dotted the surface of the altar and a groove for the sword appeared.

This is it, I thought.

Robert placed his hand on her shoulder and they shared an affectionate glance. His head bobbed up and down once.

Pulling a small piece of paper from her pocket, she recited the spell to wake The Lady of the Lake, and hopefully that included Nimue.

Violet raised the sword with both hands, ready to plunge the blade into the stone. Emilia was still nowhere in sight. I needed to buy us some time if my plan was going to have any chance of succeeding. With a flick of my wrist, I sent the Healer over the side of the rocks into the lake below. Violet stood frozen with the blade in her hand, staring at the spot her companion had just disappeared from.

"Hello, Violet," I greeted her with a curious smile.

"Morgana," she seethed, still holding the sword above her head. "You can't stop me. I will wake her." She lifted the blade a little higher, ready to plunge it into the stone.

All in good time, I thought.

"You speak of her as if she's an actual person." I paced back and forth, my dress trailing behind me with each turn.

"Regardless of what she is, I will wake her, and she will send you back to hell."

A low chuckle rumbled in my chest. She had spirit; I liked that about her. But she was new to the world of Magic, which made her naïve.

"You really don't know, do you?"

"Stop playing games, Morgana." She inched the sword toward the stone. Her hands shook from the power calling to Excalibur.

Where the devil are you, Emilia?

"The Lady," I continued to stall, "is not a woman. She's an entity you must take within yourself. She'll destroy you the second you release her." Her eyes danced back and forth.

"You're lying." Her emotions betrayed her false bravado as the truth of the situation settled over her.

"You know something, don't you?" I stepped closer. "Someone warned you." Her eyes focused on mine and I reached my hand toward her.

"That's close enough," she warned. Lifting the sword, she pointed it at me instead of the stone. "What do you care if waking her does kill me?"

"Do you really have no regard for your own life?" I took a step back, keeping her focus on me.

"Again, I don't see how that's any of your concern."

A familiar sensation passed through me, and I couldn't help but smile.

"You've done your part, played out your destiny beautifully," I beamed. "But I'm afraid this is the end of the line for you."

Emilia appeared in front of us, bowing her head as she faced me, a little worse for the wear.

"I'll take it from here," she said.

Violet looked between Emilia and me, confusion wrinkling her face. "Why do you want to wake The Lady? I thought she was meant to destroy you?"

"Whoever said I was going to wake *her*?" My eyebrows rose playfully, and I couldn't help but smirk. So much planning had gone into this moment; finally, Nimue was just a few breaths away.

"If not The Lady, then who?"

"Nimue. The other half of her soul, of course."

"Yeah, well, I was born for this," Violet retorted.

She lifted the sword and plunged it into the rock. Bright yellow light erupted from the stones as raw, hot Magic coursed up the blade and into her hands.

"Stop her," I yelled over the roar of Magic.

Emilia burst through the light, hitting Violet square in the chest with a Disarming Spell and throwing her backward, away from the altar. Relief washed over me as Emilia reached for the sword and recited the final spell to call upon the Shadowlands. The brilliant light that had surrounded Violet turned stormy and dark as Emilia's fingers curled around the hilt of the sword.

"No!" Violet yelled.

Emilia let out an ear-splitting scream and fell to her knees, her hand still tightly wrapped around the hilt of the sword.

Violet sprinted toward the altar, but I was faster. Nothing could stop us now, especially not someone as pitiful as Violet Evans.

Summoning a stunning spell, she lobbed it at me, and I easily deflected the offensive spell.

"Your part is done, Waker," I spat. A quiet anger replaced my calm, even demeanor.

"Morgana, please!" Emilia screamed. Her voice was ragged and deep.

We both turned to look at the altar. Emilia's eyes had turned red, her hair completely stripped of color.

"No!" I hurried to her side. "Fight it, you can do this." I lifted her head in my hands. She couldn't give up now, not after everything we've gone through to get to this point.

A disarming spell broke Emilia's grip on the sword, and her body skidded across the smooth surface of the stones. She was alive, but just barely.

Rising to my full height, I put myself between the altar and The Waker. If we couldn't have Nimue, she couldn't have Vivian.

Summoning a cinder orb in each hand, she ran directly at me.

Throwing my arms to the side, black smoke crawled out of me like extra limbs. She lifted her shield automatically and threw the first Cinder orb.

Displacing myself, the Orb passed right through the spot I'd been standing and crashed into the rocks.

Taking her chance, Violet ran toward the sword. As she reached the altar, her fingers lunged for the hilt. Releasing a bolt of raw Magic directly at her defenseless back, I took her down with a clean hit. The time for playing nice was over.

She tumbled forward, hitting the ground so hard I was sure she wouldn't find the strength to pull herself upright.

She rolled onto her side as I stepped closer. This was it, one more spell, and The Waker would be no more.

Propping herself up, she reached for the sword again.

Tossing her away from the altar, I planted my boot on her

chest and shoved her back to the ground. "I'm so sick of people getting in my way." The roar of the wind and Magic flowing out of the stone around us was almost deafening, but I'd already been to hell and back and nothing would stop me from completing my mission.

Violet grabbed my foot with both hands, trying to dislodge herself and still defeat me. But it was too late.

As I summoned the spell that would end Violet for good, a volcanic rush of energy hit me square in the chest, throwing me off balance and sending me tumbling across the boulders.

"No," I growled as Violet wrapped her fingers around the hilt. Light exploded from the rock, engulfing Violet and the sword as I shielded my eyes.

As the light faded, the outline of a woman came into view. It was Violet's form, but I'd recognize that smirk anywhere.

"Hello, Morgana." Her voice sounded awkward and stiff.

Slowly, I got to my feet and dusted myself off.

"Vivian," I sneered.

"You shouldn't have come back to the land of the living," Vivian said with Violet's voice.

I chuckled. "And what are *you* going to do about it? Merlin's been dust for centuries. Without him, you'll have a hard time stopping me."

Vivian smiled, and a chill ran through me.

"Merlin is bound to this universe until the day it ceases to exist. I will find him, and we will send you back beyond The Veil."

I threw my hands up and hurled a wall of fire at Vivian. Without flinching, Vivian lifted the sword and deflected the flames around her. Raising the other hand, she shot a pulse of white light directly at me. The flames and the light hit each other and exploded.

Flying backward, we landed in the thick grass below.

Getting to my feet, I stood over Vivian's prone body. She wasn't used to the land of the living just yet.

"Mark my words, I will send you back to your realm and make sure you're never able to return." I let myself be taken by the wind when I heard a familiar voice whisper my name.

"Nimue?"

I froze and looked around the clearing. Violet's cohorts were running toward her. Smoke left a haze across the open field and the shadows began to multiply.

Violet may have succeeded in her quest, but so did I.

THANK YOU!

I hope you enjoyed *Le Fay*. Morgana was so much fun to write and I can't wait for you to see where she is leading us. Getting to play the bad guy for a bit was such a nice change of pace. I really love her character and just how complex she is. I hope you did too.

I'm sure you're wondering what happens next and how this is all going to play out. Will Morgana win in the end? Is Nimue back? Is Violet lost to The Lady? What about Robert and Violet's love story? Don't worry, everything will be answered in, Elysium!

On the next page you can read the first chapter of Elysium, or you can go ahead and buy the next book at your favorite retailer or directly from me on my website, allisonsipe.com

I love to hear from my readers, so please feel free to email me any questions or just drop me a line and say hello on my website, allisonsipe.com And again, thank you for taking this journey with Violet and Robert!

THANK YOU!

Until next time, Embrace Your Magic!

INTRODUCING ELYSIUM

The final installment of the Soothsayer Series is here! Enjoy a free sample on the next page and pick up your copy today!

VIOLET IN THE DARK

My hold on reality blurs as the outside world becomes fuzzy and distant.

A heavy pressure squeezes my body like I'm being forced into a tiny box.

Fear prickles through me...

I don't want to go...I push against the darkness.

I don't want to die.

CHAPTER 1

VIVIAN

Puffy, over-stuffed storm clouds moved across the sun, throwing a shadow over the lake that made gooseflesh rise on my skin. The surface of the water shifted from a calm sapphire blue to a dark midnight black. This battle was far from over. The wind picked up, rustling the hair off my face as Robert's eyes searched for his Violet.

"I... it's too hard-" Violet's words were barely a whisper in my head as the sensation of her essence faded into the background. She should have died upon waking me, but still she held on. What strength she must have to accomplish such a feat.

"It's really you, Milady?" Robert said, clearing his throat. A sharp pain shuttered through my heart as Violet's emotions warred within me. Robert looked as if someone had let the air out of him as his eyes traced my face. Realization dawning on him that Violet was no longer the woman standing before him.

"Yes. Violet succeeded in her quest to wake me," I supplied.

"I thought... I didn't realize..." his Adam's apple bobbed up and down as he let out a shaky breath.

"That I'd take on the body of The Waker?" It's an unfortunate part of the process that always leaves loved ones confused and feeling betrayed. "Your Violet is strong and though I don't know how she's survived, she has." I tried my best to reassure him again.

"How can I be sure you're telling the truth?" His fingers twitched like he wanted to touch me, but thought better of it.

"You're bonded, are you not?" I asked, as an unfamiliar thrill of Magic unfurled in the pit of my stomach.

His eyes widen for a fraction of a second. Surprise washed across his face that I was aware of their connection.

"We are," he blurted, composing himself.

"You understand, your *Artognou Magic* can only be accessed if both parties are alive?"

Understanding flickered across his features as he squared his shoulders. He held my gaze and his fingers curled into a fist as I waited to feel the connection between them.

"I see." Robert kept his eyes averted from mine.

I'd met bonded pairs before and been close to their Magic on numerous occasions, but I've never experienced the raw, unbound nature of the bond for myself.

The wind rustled my hair as the tall grass moved against my trousers. Gooseflesh crawled across my skin as every nerve in my body fired at once.

The raw, untamed Magic poured through me, taking my breath away. It was unlike anything I'd ever experienced before, warm, powerful, and hungry. It tasted like pure freedom.

Robert took a step toward me and reached for my hand; Violet let him take my fingers as another wave of energy pulsed through me at his touch. The heat began to crawl up my skin from where his hand held mine, and Violet's strength pushed me toward him.

"Violet," he breathed. "Don't give up." His thumb traced a circle on the back of my hand.

"I won't," she replied. Violet's words pierced through my head as if she was standing right next to me.

Tearing my hand from his grasp, I tapped into my Magic, shutting them out and fortifying my claim on this body.

My stomach turned as Violet faded into the background once more. I hated silencing her, but there was much to be done and I couldn't afford the distraction.

This will be rather interesting, I thought, as another sharp pain flashed across my chest.

"Your bond is young, untested." I kept my Magic close to the surface. "But strong."

A heaviness settled over my heart as Violet's spirits fell.

"Forgive me, Milady." Robert inclined his head as the last shred of their Magic dissipated within me.

"There's no need to stand on ceremony, Vivian will do."

Robert squeezed his eyes closed and exhaled. "Will Violet make it out of this?"

I studied the sharp edge of his jaw, the tension in his shoulders, uncertain of what I should tell him. Not a single person had survived this long, but the reality of her death, while she was still so close, would be too hard for him to accept. That much I knew from experience.

Robert opened his mouth to speak but was cut off by someone yelling his name.

"Robert! Oh, thank God, I was worried you…" a woman came to a stop next to him, her brow furrowing as she took in the pained look on his face. "What's wrong? Did you guys find The Lady?" She turned to look at me and her eyes widened.

"Violet?" She squared her shoulders as her eyes held mine.

"Brett, meet The Lady of the Lake." Robert motioned between Brett and myself.

Brett's head swiveled to look at Robert, and she whispered, "What happened?"

Sparks danced up and down my fingers as my eyes

caught three figures jogging across the open field toward us. "Do they belong to you as well?" I asked, taking a step forward.

"Yes," Brett shouted, "There's no need for your defenses." Her eyes fell to my hands and I let the Magic die with one last crackle.

"Whoa, what's with the *X-Men* eyes, Violet?" One of the men joked with a playful smile.

"Ethan." The woman who shared his features nodded her head toward Brett and Robert.

Brett shot him a warning glance, and he looked at me and Robert.

"Allow me to introduce myself," I started. "The title you'll know me by is The Lady of the Lake, but you may call me Vivian."

"This is a joke, right?" The bronzed skinned woman looked at Robert for confirmation.

He folded his arms over his chest, and without looking at me, he said, "I'm afraid she speaks the truth, Elodie."

"But Violet? I mean, is she...?" The tall, broad shoulder man asked.

"Jake," Brett scolded the man.

"In my experience," I interjected. "The host is destroyed upon my entry, but Violet has survived within this body."

Everyone looked at each other, fidgeting and trying not to stare as I spoke.

"And Morgana?" Jake asked.

"She's escaped, for now." Anger bloomed in my chest, hot and furious.

"We need to get out of here before they regroup," Brett recommended.

"Where's Lila and Annabel?" Jake searched the group for their face.

"Lila didn't make it," Robert said.

Again, Violet's emotions bubbled to the surface and guilt pierced through me.

"I'm sorry, brother, Lila was complicated, but I know you cared for her."

"Jake, there's something you need to know about, Annabel." Robert's voice broke, and he couldn't meet his brother's eyes.

"Not here." Brett grabbed Robert's arm.

"Putting it off, won't make it any easier." Robert whirled on Brett. "He should know."

"Tell me." Jake's eyes darted between Robert and Brett.

"Annabel." Robert closed the gap between him and Jake and placed a hand on his brother's shoulder. "She's gone."

"What're you — no." Jake shook his head and stepped away from Robert.

"She's been gone a long time," Robert continued. "Since the day Ian took her."

"No, no, we got her back, we saved her." Jake's brow furrowed and his hands balled into fists.

"The woman parading as your wife showed us her true form and killed Lila right in front of us." Robert's voice was devoid of emotion.

A flash of a memory skirted through my mind. A blonde woman shifting into a redhead. A blade across another woman's neck and Violet's hands covered in the victim's blood as she held her.

Brett stepped forward like she was approaching a wild animal and said, "Ian told us, our Annabel, the real Annabel," she hesitated. "Was killed by his hand the day he took her."

"No," Jake argued. "Why would they take her, if they were just going to kill her, why? It doesn't make sense," he yelled at no one in particular.

"I don't—"

"You're wrong," Jake growled at Brett.

I stepped forward, wanting to help him see the truth of their words. Reaching out my hand, my fingers brushed against Jake's temple. A rush of Magic coursed through my torso and Violet's memory played between us. The woman playing his wife slit Lila's throat, then shifted from Annabel to her true form.

Jake's eyes met mine for a fraction of a second. I watched the heartbreak work its way from his chest and into his eyes as his knees hit the soft earth.

Looking down at his hands as if he was staring at Annabel, he uttered her name softly and I could feel the tiny cracks in Violet's heart open up. She knew pain and loss all too well, it would seem.

"I'm so sorry," Brett whispered. Kneeling next to Jake, she wrapped her arms around his shoulders.

"I too am sorry for your loss." I took a step toward them. "But we must move to a more convenient location."

"No," Jake barked. His face contorted into a mask of pain and anger. "I held her in my arms, cared for her, loved her."

"You didn't know," Robert argued. "None of us did."

"I should have known," Jake shouted as his eyes filled with tears. "I should have—"

"Stop, you can't do this to yourself. Anna wouldn't want you to blame yourself." Brett gripped Jake's shoulder.

Jake's eyes met hers as a tear trailed down his cheek. "If it was Matty, you'd blame yourself, wouldn't you?" He snapped.

Brett's mouth opened and closed.

"It's not my wish to rush your grieving, but we must take our leave in the event Morgana returns," I said again.

"I need to… bring Lila home." Robert moved away from the group through the tall, thick grass, and Brett pulled Jake to his feet. Following Robert, the others whispered among themselves as I scanned the open field. The chill that hung in the air was more than just the weather turning. I could feel the darkness in my bones with each step I took. Something was lurking out there, something sinister and not of this world.

Robert came to a stop, and the others halted a few feet away, giving him the space he needed. As he knelt down in the grass, I moved toward him, pushing past the others. Lila's body was no more. Only a pile of black ash remained on the blades of grass.

Robert laid his hand on the ash, the glint of something silver catching my eye.

"I'm so sorry," he said under his breath.

I knelt next to Robert, placing my hand on top of his and said, "Whether you brought happiness or pain, may your soul yet win delights on this, your death-day."

"Thank you," Robert said, without looking at me. His fingers pushed the ashes aside, and he picked up the silver ring and stuffed it in his pocket.

"It's not safe here," I reminded him. "We need to seek shelter." I scanned the dark clouds holding steadfast to the horizon.

Nodding his head, he stood and turned to face his family. "Let's go home," he said.

I held my hand out for him to grab.

"For those of you who wish to return," I held out my other hand. "Robert, if you'll please picture home in your mind." I nodded to him.

Ethan and Elodie grabbed onto my arm while Brett and Jake held onto Robert.

The Magic inside me unfurled like a rose blooming, slow and easy. *"Auferetur."*

Within the blink of an eye, we were home, wherever home was for Robert and his comrades.

A dizzy spell washed over me as I took in the furnishings. It felt like someone had taken hold of my intestine with a death grip. I could feel Violet more prominently again as the edges of my vision blurred.

"They're back," a voice shouted, and a pair of arms wrapped around me.

"Jake? Jake, what's wrong?" A worried female voice called after him.

"It's been a long day. Leave him," Robert said.

"We'll go." Ethan nodded and he and Elodie followed Jake.

"Thank God you're safe." A tiny woman with short dark hair held me at arm's length, then let go of me like a hot coal.

The pain in my abdomen sharpened, and I slumped against the wall, letting out a heavy breath. Holding out my hands, they shook as I turned them over.

"Are you okay?" Robert grabbed my elbow to steady me.

"Of course." I cleared my throat. "Just out of practice."

"Is this normal?" Violet's voice rang in my head.

"Nothing about this is normal," I replied.

"Vivian, is that you?" A familiar, gentle voice said from somewhere above me.

"By the stars. It's you." An overwhelming sense of relief washed over me.

"Ahh, my dear Vivian. It's been quite a long time. I was afraid you wouldn't recognize me."

"You two know each other?" Robert's eyes caught mine and his brow furrowed as he tried to work out how I could know anyone in his world.

"You could say that." I shrugged and took a ragged breath.

"Your face may have changed," I said through another spout of dizziness, "But you can't hide the stench of your Magic." I did my best to hide the pain in my voice as Violet grew stronger.

"Good to see, The Lady of The Lake still has a sense of humor." He held his arms out to me.

"You and I both know I was always the humorous one, Merlin." I stepped into the circle of his arms and my legs went out from under me as darkness fell over my eyes.

ACKNOWLEDGMENTS

First and foremost, I must thank my family and friends for their support on this journey. The Soothsayer world has become a huge part of my life and you guys let me share all my crazy, hair-brained ideas with you!

Jessica, your continued support means the world to me and I'm so glad I have you to read each and every book before it goes out into the wild. Your input is invaluable and Le Fay is all the better because of you.

Eric, I am so lucky to have you in my life. You're always so willing to let me bounce ideas off of you and you pick me up when I feel like the whole thing has crumbled to pieces. You truly are my partner in crime and I can't wait to share my next crazy idea with you!

I have to give a big SHOUT OUT to 20books50K. Joining the group has been the best thing for my career. With all of the collective knowledge and support in one place, it's no wonder so many of us are finding success.

And thank you to every reader who's made it this far in the series! I absolutely love getting your emails and messages on social media. Your words encourage me every day and I don't know what I'd do without you! You guys seriously rock my socks!

ABOUT THE AUTHOR

Allison Sipe lives in Southern California with her boyfriend and two adorable dogs. She has a degree from California State University Northridge in English Literature and is very proud to have gone to school for something she loves.

When she's not reading and writing, she loves to travel. She's been around all around Europe, London is one of her favorite cities and the little island of Kauai is where she gets a lot of her writing done.

If you'd like to contact her, you can message her on her website of find her on most social media platforms.

www.allisonsipe.com